The Scientist

&

THE SQUID

A Love Story

By

Terry Perry

Dedication

This book is dedicated to Tammy whose edits took this book from mediocre to good. A good editor is hard to find and I got lucky with this one.

Forward

This book is for all of those who have loved and won. It is also for those that have loved and lost and if you are one that has lost, never give up, there is always someone out there for you; you just haven't found them yet. When you do find them, your life will be fuller and richer than anything you could imagine.

As we progress into the digital age, the outlets for dating and connecting with another human being is beyond comprehension. There are dating apps galore and if a person can't find someone they are compatible with, well then, they are just not trying.

Although I'm sure that people are still meeting in bars, bowling alleys, and colleges, but this book is about how two people randomly met in an online chat room. Now if there are a thousand dating apps, there must be a million chat rooms. There are chat rooms for sports enthusiasts, car restoration gear heads, wood working carpenters, needlepoint crafters, kids, teens, men, women, gays, and lesbians. There are live chat rooms, music chat rooms, video game chat rooms, and I believe that there are even chat rooms for chat rooms. However, the focus of this novella is about two women who met in a lesbian chat room. I only selected a lesbian chat room because it is what I am most familiar. I guess I could've written about two people who fell in love in a needlepoint chat room but I don't think it would've been as dramatic or intriguing.

One is a teacher and one is a Navy veteran often called a Squid in the naval community like a Marine is called a Jarhead. One is dedicated to molding the minds of our youth and the other is dedicated to mechanical engineering. If there were ever an odd couple, it is these two. One is tall while the other is short. One is blonde and the other has brown hair. One is older, the other younger. The teacher is more right brain and enjoys the arts, fictional books, and decorating the house. The squid is totally left brain with an obsession for spreadsheets, logic, and always considered her scientific calculator to be her best friend.

This book is about how love can bridge the gaps of uncertainty. That in its truest form, love is unconditional, forgiving, understanding, and ultimately blind because The Teacher's and The Squid's destiny would forever involve feelings and emotions but only in the written form.

Enjoy!

Chapter 1

"Lynn"

Lynn coasted her bicycle through the parking lot of her job, allowing her breathing to slow down as she zigzagged back and forth, making her way to her Jeep. She had a good ride that day and considered that she was lucky to be able to spend her lunch time exercising rather than chit chatting with the other gals in the break room. It's not that she didn't enjoy her time with her co-workers, because she did, and on days when they met, laughing ensued followed by choking sounds as women inhaled their food during a riotous fit of table-pounding merriment. They couldn't help themselves as they joked and chided each other on whatever work-related dysfunction occurred that day. Some poor sap became the center of their conversation and would be verbally shredded to pieces as they dined on their sandwiches and fruit that they all shared with one another. However, Lynn felt the need to ride and clear her head of the cranial constipation that was blocking her thought processes with her latest project. She just couldn't seem to find the ebb and flow usually experienced when she was "on". She felt a little "off" and thought a ride would be the best solution for breaking through the crap that was cluttering her brain, metaphorically speaking.

She hopped off of her bike and set it in the bike rack on the back of the Jeep and began to unbuckle her helmet when she saw one of the machinists pushing Mike's car as they attempted to pop the clutch and start his car. She really liked Mike, he was the leader of a group of the machinists that worked at the company and he was smart which she found appealing in anyone, male or female. Although Mike was not her sexual preference, she still liked him and prided herself in that fact that she wasn't one of these anti-male lesbians. She had always been open minded when it came to human beings and thought that everyone has something to offer, no matter how small or how annoying. Lynn knew that all people had a purpose for being on this planet even if that purpose was not easily seen or readily experienced. She chuckled as Mike popped the clutch and the engine roared to life. He turned the car around toward the exit and yelled, "Don't ever buy a Subaru!" as he drove by her. Lynn just shook her head smiling to herself and thought, "I just gave him kudos for being smart."

Lynn loved her job and had made a career of being a Quality Manager after an 8-year stint of being in the Navy and performing Quality Assurance on Nuclear Propulsion Plants. In some aspects, it spoiled her in regards to the civilian workforce. Everyone she worked with in the Navy stepped up to the plate and gave their best every day, there were no slackers in her field because if someone made a mistake, others could die. So it was a real eye opener when she joined the civilian work force and learned that not everyone came to work every day to do the best job they could instead of just coming to work to get a paycheck. She is still taken aback at the number of people who THINK they do a good job. It took a couple of years for Lynn to learn how to adapt and adjust her attitude about working in this sector of employment and those years were sometimes turbulent and lonely, but they were always a learning experience even at the young age of 27. And learn she did, she learned to be a coach instead of an authoritarian, and she learned how to see a person's strength and help develop their weaknesses. She stifled her memories, turned to the building, hopped up the three stairs to the door, and with a swift pass of her badge, she opened the cipher door and entered.

She made her way to the women's locker room and briefly acknowledged the side eyed glances from the guys as they admired her lean and trim body. At 35, she was glad that she had continued the physical training the Navy had required of her and was pleased with her physique. Her thigh and calf muscles were well toned and sculptured from riding her bike. Her stomach was still flat and her butt tight. She felt no need to exercise her legs at the gym but focused more on her abs and upper body during her rigorous workouts three times a week. She did occasionally walk on the treadmill but this was more to watch the news rather than work out her legs. She quickly showered and put on the clothes that she wore to work that day. Taking one last look in the mirror to adjust her jeans and button down, she started to her office.

As she approached, she could see that a line had already formed outside her door. This was typical during Lynn's work day. There were always people that needed or wanted something; a document, a manual, a print or a drawing was the most requested items during her 10 hour day. She could tell by the number of people standing at attention that this day would probably turn into a

12 hour day if she had any hopes of completing her own work.

She walked down the hall and the people at the back of the line turned and began stating their requests, she quickly smiled and said, "If you wanted to be first to get helped then you should be at the head of the line."

The man closest to the door blushed when she said, "Hi Fred, how can I help you today?"

Fred quickly looked to at his shoes and turned even redder while he asked, "I need a drawing Miss Lynn."

The other guys in line immediately began to snicker because everyone in the company knew that Frank had a big crush on Lynn. Even though she was out as a lesbian at work, it never ceased to amaze her of how many straight men found her attractive and dropped subtle hints of taking her out on a date. She entered her password into her computer and Windows began to pop open on her screen, she quickly located Fred's drawing, clicked on the Printer Icon and the copy began to emerge from her printer. She stamped the drawing "Uncontrolled" and handed it to Fred and flashed him her brightest smile along with a, "Here you go". Fred turned to leave but before he left, he mumbled, "Thank you Miss Lynn." The line of guys began to laugh and someone yelled,

"Hey Fred, how many copies of that drawing do you have in your Tool Box already?"

Fred turned crimson with embarrassment and in a louder voice said, "Shut up you guys." as he quickly made his way down the hall.

Lynn leaned out her door and playfully told the others that they shouldn't tease Fred like that, he was a good worker and always produced good parts. She ended her little reprimand with, "You all could learn a lot from Fred."

One of the guys said, "Yeah, like how to ask for the same print every three days." Lynn chuckled and said, "But still, you shouldn't make fun at him." She looked at the next machinist in line and said, "Next."

It took over an hour to grant all of the requests because some people just wanted to talk and not being a rude person, Lynn listened intently to each person who came to see her. After the last one left, she looked at her watch and thought, "It's going to be a very long afternoon."

She turned to her desk and looked at the large pile of work ahead of her, drew in a deep breath and said, "No time like the present." Then she tackled her work with a vengeance. She analyzed her spreadsheets and smiled to herself when her equations and formulas were spot on and the data rang true with positive results. It was three hours before she stopped tapping her forehead and chewing on the end of her pencil as she concentrated on polynomials, sines, and cosines. She was a math addict and enjoyed nothing more than solving a complex equation. Well, she did enjoy something more than math but she quickly pushed the thought of being wrapped up in another woman's arms out of her head. She didn't have time to daydream about what was quickly becoming a seemingly impossibility right now. She never considered herself lonely, her days were filled with activity and people, and on most evenings, she dropped into bed with exhaustion. However, every once in a while, her mind would wonder what it would be like to have a hand to hold again, to have someone send her flowers, or call her just to say, *I was thinking about you.* It had been three years since her last relationship, and she was in no hurry to jump back into the dating scene. She physically felt worn out when she thought about dating again. The pomp and circumstance of meeting someone new, getting over the jitters and anxiety that came with the initial encounter, none of it appealed to her. She also knew that if she didn't endure the "getting to know you" phase, she would probably stay alone and that saddened her, but only for a minute. She had been able to train her brain to dismiss these thoughts and concentrate on the reality in front of her.

Retraining her brain had become second nature for Lynn. After growing up in an alcoholic, abusive dysfunctional home, her ability to "switch" her thought patterns was as quick as lightening. She was the second daughter born to Jack and Eileen. He was a very abusive alcoholic and she was a very abusive co-dependent. Lynn learned later that there is such a thing as a co-alcoholic. This is someone who displays the same characteristics of an alcoholic; they just don't drink. Therefore, Lynn considered her mother to be a co-alcoholic with extreme co-dependent tendencies. Having that knowledge didn't make her childhood any less forgiving because it was a nightmare from the word go.

Lynn grew up very poor, and that being said, she meant welfare-food-stamps in the projects-poor. Whatever money there was went to support her Dad's drinking habit. She wasn't born in a hospital, either. Her mom walked into the local clinic on December 8th and told them she was going to have a baby. She was so thin that they told her to come back when she had gained weight. She not-so-kindly told them that she was, "having this kid" and they had better get a doctor. She walked over, laid on a gurney and waited for someone to help her. Lynn entered the world shortly thereafter while the doctor was putting on his gown. He looked at her Mom and said, "Eileen, you've could've waited".

While her Mom argued with the doctor about delaying child birth, Lynn's first earthly needs were going unattended. As the story is told, an intern caught her before she hit the floor and stood there with this sputtering, screaming bundle of life without a clue as to what to do with it. Lynn's Mom asked for her and cleaned her up while the doctor severed the umbilical cord that tethered her to the only life force she had known for nine months. Even though Lynn thought that she was safe in her mother's womb, she needed to get out of there because a nine month diet of caffeine and nicotine is not conducive to a fetus. Her mother was a heavy smoker and would consume to the side effects of the habit within the next 29 years. Lynn's father died of a broken neck some 11 years later. Alcoholics typically die violent or tragic deaths.

Lynn was a beautiful baby, born with a glowing tan, weighing in at six pounds, three ounces. She would be the runt of her Mom's litter as compared to the weight of her siblings. For most of her childhood, she considered herself to be adopted because her brain didn't think like the other members of the family. What she experienced, the things that she saw and heard just didn't make sense to her; Lynn always thought, "There has to be a better way". And even though she couldn't comprehend that the life she was living was dysfunctional, it would become the better part of her existence. Let's face it; breaking the chains of dysfunction is just fucking hard.

There were no pictures taken of Lynn at her birth. This is another event that perpetuated her thoughts of adoption. According to her Mom, she brought Lynn home and the baby was a sickly little thing. Her mother would tell her of a story that on the third day of being on this planet, she developed

14

colic and wouldn't stop crying. This angered her father who was nursing a hangover and as the story is told, he spanked her. Now what normal, rational, loving parent spanks a newborn? Lynn's mind doesn't remember this event but she does remember not crying at his funeral. As time progressed, living with her father was turbulent and violent. The only things that she inherited from her father were his nose and the ability to consume mass quantities of alcohol on a frequent basis. Lynn would later quit drinking but not before circumnavigating her own paths of destruction.

Her Mom was a story teller, not as good as her grandmother, but she was prolific when it came to telling stories of Lynn's birth, and the story was told quite often, if not merely for the fact to make Lynn feel guilty for entering this world or to scare the shit out of her. In hindsight, her Mother was successful at both. What child would not feel the insidious tentacles of guilt upon learning the extreme pain and sacrifice their mother endured to give them life? Yes, her Mom was a regular Edgar Allan Poe and sent Lynn to bed many a night in tears of horror and self-loathing. Lynn would sit on her little stool in her grandmother's warm kitchen and listen to stories that no child should hear until they had reached an age of understanding to learn that the tales were just stories and couldn't hurt them. But at the time, her little brain couldn't comprehend the magnitude of how her grandfather killed himself with a shotgun, which was another Mom favorite.

Lynn must have been around a year old when she began pulling herself up on furniture and learning to walk. Now in those days, her grandmother didn't have air conditioning and her method of cooling her shot gun style house was a big ass window fan in the front room blowing air in and another big ass window fan in the back room sucking air out. This created somewhat of a vacuum that could cause a toddler to learn how to run before they learned how to walk. It just sucked anything in its path from the front of the house to rear, even little children. Now as the story goes, Lynn's uncle had his tool box underneath the fan in the back room. As the adults in the house were more concerned with contemplating their disastrous white trash kind of life, no one was watching out for Lynn. She grabbed the bottom edge of the fan with her left hand, pulled her little unstable self up onto the tool box and in doing so, her right hand went into the fan and the metal blades mangled her tiny fingers. The self-absorbed adults heard the screams and came running to see what the commotion was all about. After finding her, Lynn's Mom wrapped her little hand in a bath towel and her Uncle Joe sped them off to the hospital in his semi tractor trailer truck. This was the only vehicle at the house at the time. Lynn's grandmother would tell her that this was a tragic accident and that she looked for her little fingers for a very long time after her mom and uncle left the house. As an adult, Lynn doesn't reflect upon this event as an accident, someone should've been watching her and what she was doing, but growing up in a dysfunctional home means that children are invisible and are more of an annoyance than a joy.

She spent 4 hours in surgery as her pediatrician stitched up the little fingers. No fingers were lost but they became bent and crooked and still are to this day. Though she is right handed, Lynn grew up being ashamed of her most used phalanges. She ended up with over 200 stitches in her hand and scars for life. Even though the "accident" happened at her grandmother's house, they actually lived in the projects. The projects consist of low income tenement housing of which all look alike and can also be referred to as the "ghetto", the "hood", or the "East Bottoms" of Kansas City. Due to the filth and decay of their living conditions, the doctor would not let Lynn come home from the hospital until the stitches were out and the hand had healed a little bit. So she remained at Children's Mercy Hospital for two weeks on a children's ward for kids ranging in age from one to twelve. Her Mom would come to the hospital and watch her through the round window that looked out onto the ward as Lynn sat and ate a carrot with the cook that prepared their meals. Or she would find Lynn with a book following around this boy who knew how to read. Lynn was not allowed to see her lest she became upset and wanted to go home with her.

Fourteen days and a couple of hundred stitches later, Lynn went home to begin her physical therapy which consisted of her father working out the stiffness and rigidity of her little hand. It was the only honorable thing that he ever did for her. He would hold out his fingers, Lynn would grab hold of them, and he would lift her off of the ground in order to build the strength in her fingers. For this she thanked him.

Lynn took a moment and looked down at her hand, it was still damaged but she had grown up with her fingers looking a certain way. She was just grateful that it hadn't happened to her left hand. One day she would like to have a ring on that hand given to her by someone that had captured her heart. But that wasn't going to happen today.

However, little did Lynn know that her life was about to change dramatically in the very near future. A woman was about to enter her world in a big way and Lynn would have to re-evaluate her purpose. Nothing prepared her for the electronic encounter she was about to experience and it would baffle her. Her routine days and evenings would no longer go as planned and she would find herself impatiently waiting to see if she had mail from a certain screen name in a chat room.

Chapter 2

"High Anxiety"

Lynn looked out her bedroom window and dismally noticed the rivulets of rain running down the pane. Winters in New England were brutal and seemed interminable. They never seemed to end and spring couldn't get here soon enough. It was going to be another soaker of a day which meant she couldn't ride her bike at lunch so it looked like a lunch date with the girls. She put the curtain back and headed for the shower. She loved her showers, feeling the hot water cascade down her body always relaxed her and invigorated her at the same time. Plus, she liked the clean feeling that a long shower always seemed to provide. She soaped up her sponge and gently cleaned her body from the tips of her fingers to her toes. She liked the way the bubbles looked against her tanned skin as the hot water pulsed against her back. She rinsed all of the soap from her body, turned the water off and reached for her towel.

With the towel still wrapped around her, she padded out to the kitchen to get her first cup of coffee of the day. She considered coffee her only vice and silently thought, "I really need to cut back on this stuff, but it's so good." She drank her coffee with cream and fake sweetener in the morning, a cup of black Joe in the afternoon, and another cup with cream and sweetener in the afternoon. She loved her coffee and thought that there were worse vices to have. She took her coffee and made her way back to her bedroom to get dressed. She flipped through her wardrobe and settled on a pink and white pinstripe button down and her favorite Roper blue jeans. She pulled out a pair of black socks and her charcoal grey, boiled wool work shoes. Working in a machine shop environment meant oil on the floor most of the time so all of her work shoes were non-slip as required by company policy. She liked all of her work shoes and had different colors that matched her shirts. She had a pair of burgundy shoes that would go with the pink shirt but decided on the grey to match the weather. She quickly dressed, slipped into her shoes and made her way back to the bathroom to brush her hair and begin her morning routine. She brushed her teeth, rubbed her face with her favorite cream, took her vitamin and put her diamond studs in her pierced ear lobes.

She liked her diamonds. They were only a quarter carat but they were dainty and sparkled brilliantly when the light hit them, plus they added a feminine touch to her ensemble. She missed dressing up but her work environment wasn't conducive to dresses and skirts, besides, she would look ridiculous in a dress and her work shoes. The ladies in the office wore dresses and skirts but she didn't work on the carpet side of the building. Speaking of the ladies, she needed to make her lunch because she would be joining them for lunch on this rainy day.

Lynn opened the fridge and perused the contents, looking for something quick and easy to prepare. She settled on a chicken lettuce wrap, a non fat plain yogurt, and blueberries. She hauled out the chicken salad, the lettuce, and tortillas. She quickly assembled her wrap, rolled it up in aluminum foil and threw it in her lunch bag, followed by the yogurt and blueberries. She grabbed an apple and a string cheese for snacks just in case she needed them. She poured her coffee into a to-go cup, found her purse and headed for the door, ready to begin another day. She opened the door and quickly determined that an umbrella was required if she didn't want to get wet when she walked to her Jeep. She pulled an umbrella out of the stand, popped it open and briskly walked to her car. She slid into the driver's seat and put her purse and lunch bag in the passenger seat. She thought to herself about how nice it would be to be handing her things to a lovely lady sitting in that same seat. She closed her eyes and shook the thought out of her head. These were just crazy thoughts but they kept creeping in at the most inopportune times. She started the Jeep and backed out of the driveway, pointed it east and drove to work.

There was another line of people formed outside of her office, not as daunting as the line from yesterday and she quickly scanned the crowd, Frank was not in attendance. This gave her hope; she was in a cranky mood due to the rain but smiled at the guys in line in spite of herself. Counting her blessings, this entourage only added a half hour to her day. She cringed at the amount of people would be there after lunch. As she sat her purse down, her phone rang. She looked down and the caller ID said that the President of the company was on the line. Her heart sank; this could only mean bad news. Stan only called her when a customer needed pacifying or a major return of product was about to happen. She picked up both the phone and her own voice, sounding cheery, she said, "Good morning Stan, how can I help you?" Stan had her on speaker phone which meant that she needed to stay upbeat, helpful, and refrain from any jokes because one never knew if there were others in the room. Stan immediately began talking about a problem with one of the customers that fell under the huge canopy of Department of Defense. Stan spouted, "Lynn, this account has big, I mean big potential and we can't afford for there to be a problem with Hanscomb. I need you to go over to their facility and get to the root of this". Lynn was already nodding her head in agreement. She inquired, "How big of a problem is there?" Stan replied, "This could blow up in our face so get over there and fix this mess!"

Lynn no longer reported to the President, she was moved under the Operations Leader when the new guy was hired but it didn't matter, when Stan said, "Jump!" most people within hearing distance asked, "How High?" Not that he was a tyrant, because he wasn't, he was just the kind of leader that people wanted to follow. He was a young President and placed great value on family, community, courtesy, and continuous improvement. Lynn liked that about him and always felt honored when he asked something of her. She debated as to whether to power up her pc and check her mail before she headed over to the customer's location. She quickly decided that it would be worth it and she hit the Control, Alt, Delete buttons. The computer hummed to life with clicks, beeps, and whirrs, she clicked on the Outlook Icon and the emails started scrolling in, not a bad morning for content. There were no correspondences blatantly in need of attention; the Finance Manager posted the Sales and Orders to date, those numbers seemed to be as dismal as the weather. She grabbed her purse then sat it back down and thought she needed to check in with her "real" boss before she just took off and picked up the phone again. She dialed Derek's extension and he picked up on the second ring with a, "Good Morning Lynn." Lynn quickly gave him a summary of her previous conversation with Stan and said that she needed to go over to Hanscomb's and see what the problem was and that she would keep him posted. He replied, "Let me know if you need someone to go with you." She said, "I'm just going over to assess the situation, I should be back shortly and I'll come see you." Derek replied, "Good deal, see you when you get back."

Lynn picked up her purse again, checked out with Jake, her Department "Lead" and made her way back to her Jeep. Jake was a good Lead and had been working for her for the last two years and she liked him. In fact, she had recruited an exceptional group of talent in her department and was proud of each one of them. They worked great as a team but could also hold their own independently. She never worried when she was off site because she knew that they would work just fine without her. She walked through the Production Center on her way to the door. She saw Frank and he nodded hello as she quickly walked around the machines. Lynn nodded back and gave him a "Good Morning" smile and a nod back. As she walked through the Warehouse, the Shipping/Receiving Lead said, "Are you leaving so soon, you just got here?" The Warehouse was currently another department that fell under her responsibility and for the last two months, she was doing two jobs. She had to let go of the previous Warehouse Manager for poor performance and it still nagged at her because they had become friends. She made a mental note, "Never become friends with direct reports." She had friends at work, like the women in the front office, but none of them reported directly to her so she was confident that the "Lunch Bunch" was safe from any undue influence that could possibly come from

26

her. She quickly waved to the Lead and yelled, "I'll be back soon."

Lynn opened her umbrella as she left the building. The rain was still coming down but the wind had died and that was a good sign. It was still cool and she was glad that she hadn't had time to take off her pull over when she was in her office.

She slid back into the driver's seat of her Jeep and said a silent, "Thank goodness." because the Jeep had not had a chance to cool down while she was in the building. She turned the ignition and drove to the exit, one left turn and a stop light later, she entered the on ramp to Route 3 and began her drive to Hanscomb's. It wasn't a long drive over to the customer but she quickly became lost in her thoughts. One of her favorite songs came on the radio and she found herself daydreaming again about having someone special in her life. The song playing led her mind to a place in her consciousness in which there was a woman that was completely opposite of Lynn but had captured her heart. The song sang of a woman that was always late to get ready to go out; loved to dance and take chances; would make plans to go out on the weekend but decided to stay home on the couch. Lynn liked this song because it sang of the epitome of everything Lynn wasn't. She was always on time if not early, she had two left feet when it came to dancing but to her credit, she could move her hips to the rhythm of most any song, and when she made plans, she usually kept those plans. Lynn chuckled to herself as she listened to the tune thinking that it would be her luck to have someone in her life that would have minimal characteristics in common with her. As she listened, she began to sing the lyrics with a small smile on her face and let her mind go to that place that she usually kept locked in an iron grip.

In her mind's eye, Lynn envisioned a pretty woman changing multiple outfits to wear on their date because she just couldn't make up her mind as to which one would be the best for the occasion. Her fictitious girlfriend would come down stairs looking like a million bucks and ask, "How's this?" Lynn would think, "Wow, you're a knock out!" With that said, the woman would turn and go back upstairs to find something else to wear. Lynn would think to herself with a smile, "We are going to be so late." But also knew that it would be so worth it when her date finally found the right outfit. Not wanting the daydream to end, she let her mind continue with the words of the song and saw the gorgeous woman dancing. Lynn's vision finds a woman in her element on the dance floor. Her date was a heart ache on the dance floor; she moved like smoke and was comfortable dancing alone, lost in the music, breaking hearts with every move. In Lynn's pretend date all she could think was, "My goodness, that girl is mine." Lynn looked up just in time to take her exit and quickly gasped, "Oh no, that was close, if I don't pay attention, I could end up in Maine!" she laughed at herself for her absentmindedness.

Lynn took a minute to regroup and switch gears in her mind from her lovely daydream to her purpose at hand as she pulled her Jeep into the Visitor's parking space. She said a silent prayer that the man that she was supposed to see was in a good mood. Bill Turtle could be cantankerous at times. Bill Turtle was not his real name but it's what everyone called him because he moved his head up and down and he was slow to respond, just like a turtle. Also like a turtle, he stayed on a given path and could be tenacious with a problem and relentless until he received a suitable resolution.

She opened her door, climbed out of the Jeep with ID in hand. Being a provider to the Department of Defense, Hanscomb's had a strict security policy and checking in reminded Lynn of joining the Navy. They wanted every detail down to the name of the first born in the family. Although annoying, Lynn understood the purpose of high security, especially for a company that supplied munitions directly to the US Army. After the attack on the US on 9/11, one could not be too careful. Lynn still remained patriotic and believed that there was no better country to live in than the good ole US of A. She loved this country and it was an honor to serve it during her youth, a time when she was still innocent and truly believed that she was serving a purpose and willing to die for that purpose. She still got misty when she heard Taps played on a bugle. She took her Visitor badge from the guard and patiently waited for Bill Turtle.

Bill arrived and Lynn noticed that he was still wearing polyester pants and white sneakers. He was such a nerd she thought playfully. As he said, "Good Morning", Lynn knew that her silent prayer had been answered; Bill was in a good mood. In his distinct deadpan voice he said, "I'm so glad you could come so quickly." She replied, "Of course Bill, Hanscomb's problems are our problems and I hope that I can help." Bill led her up the stairs past the employee break room and noticed the size of the room and that it contained individual tables and chairs. It looked like the food court in a mall and the smells exuding from it were enticing even at this hour of the morning. She compared it to her own company's break room and wished that they had invested in tables and chairs instead of the folding picnic table type furniture they sat at when they at their lunch. The front office had a small break room with a high table and chairs, a nice stainless steel microwave and fridge with an ice dispenser. The office break room could set 3 people comfortably, maybe 4, but any bodies over four or five found it cramped and elbows were known to hit each other during the mid day meal.

As she and Bill entered the Inspection Room, Lynn noticed how small the room was and that they didn't have nearly the sophisticated measuring devices that ACME Machining had invested. She always thought that her company's name was rather lame and it reminded her of the old Roadrunner and Coyote cartoons from the 1960's. Wiley E. Coyote was always buying some kind of high powered rocket from ACME in order to catch the Roadrunner. The Coyote usually ended up being flattened to a canyon wall or dropping to the bottom in some kind of tragic accident. He never caught the Roadrunner. Bill led her to a bench that contained several totes with bags of parts in each tote. Lynn began to frown, "This was a lot of product to be nonconforming", she thought to herself. She picked up a bag of parts and asked Bill what he thought was the problem? In his best turtle motion, he nodded his head up and down, and said, "The threads don't go all of the way to thread relief and the parts won't seat correctly when they are assembled." Lynn said, "Let's have a look shall we?" She took a handful of parts and walked over to the microscope. Adjusting the sight, she could immediately see the problem and Turtle Bill was correct, the thread was just shy of the relief.

By the look of the amount of bags, Lynn deduced that there was at least 30,000 parts that were defective. This was going to be a massive return and the monetary value was staggering. This would turn out to be the largest return of her time with the company and she could feel her anxiety reach a level that she hadn't experienced since the Navy when she experienced a quasi nuclear meltdown.

She was stationed at Submarine Base Pearl Harbor during her high anxiety moment and her work center was scheduled to monitor a Resin Discharge evolution in which radioactive resin, that was used to cool the rods of the reactor, was recovered from the sub so that clean resin could be pumped back onboard. It was like a proverbially oil change for a nuclear reactor. During this particular work, it was Lynn's job to sit on top of the sub while it was in dry dock and monitor an Ultrasound machine so she could radio the engine room when there was air in the pipe in order for the pumping could cease and prevent the HEPA filter in the system from disintegrating. If air passed through the pipe, the HEPA filter would basically melt and the predicted possibility of airborne contamination would occur. After 18 hours of sitting on top of the sub from six that morning to midnight, Lynn needed a break. She made her leave from the ship and walked back to her building to use the head (bathroom) and grab a cup of coffee; she wasn't going to be relieved until six the next morning. Even with the trade winds, she was grateful for the air conditioning when she entered her spaces. She immediately headed down the passageway to the head to relieve her bladder. She sat down on the commode and nothing happened. She had been holding her pee for so long that it didn't want to evacuate her body as quickly as she wanted it to. She stood up, zipped up her dungarees, stepped out of the stall, and turned on a faucet. Running water always did the trick as she felt the urge to urinate. It was really a hardship when she was stationed aboard ship. She could go to the bathroom and as soon as she stepped out on the deck and saw the ocean, she had to do an immediate about face and return back to the head to relieve herself yet once again. It happened every morning and could be quite frustrating especially if she was running a little late. Well, late on her terms because she was never late. Even after a night on the town, she always made it to muster on time. She began to pee and experienced that wonderful feeling of bladder relief. She stood up, tucked her chambray shirt into her dungarees, zipped, and turned to flush the toilet. She exited the stall and returned to the sink to wash her hands. The water was still running, she had forgotten all about it and cursed herself for being wasteful. She washed her hands and splashed water on her face. The image in the mirror looked tired and she noticed the bags beginning to form under her eyes.

Lynn grabbed a cup of coffee and started the long walk back to the dry dock. She liked working on ships that were in dry dock.

She found it amazing that man had invented a huge box with big wooden blocks that would sink into the harbor and allow a submarine to park on the blocks and then have the water drain out like a gigantic bathtub for ships. She could see the bright lights of the dry dock to her left; it looked like a Friday night football game that she remembered from high school. There were workers everywhere, bustling back and forth from the sub to the pier, carrying tools and equipment. They reminded her of an ant farm that she once had in grade school. The little ants could be seen scurrying through the tunnels, carrying who knows what, back to the queen. In this instance, the sub was the queen and the ants were shipboard workers and other sailors going about their business. To her right, Lynn could see the lights of Honolulu twinkling in the distance and imagined all of the tourists wearing their newly purchased Hawaiian floral shirts, Bermuda shorts, and cameras slung around their necks. All of them were burnt to a crisp because everyone knows that people only come to Hawaii to get a tan. They complete their tourist outfits with white socks and sandals. This always made Lynn laugh. However, right now, she would welcome a Hawaiian Shirt, Bermuda shorts, white socks and sandals if it meant that she didn't have to climb back on top of that sub. Maybe not the white socks and sandals, even she had her standards, regardless of how tired she was.

When she returned to her position on the sub, she immediately noticed that someone had moved her UT Machine. The transducer was still taped to the pipe within the hot zone boundary but it was disconnected from the machine. This frustrated Lynn, it meant that she would have to recalibrate the machine so reached inside the ditty bag, pulled out the calibration pipe. For all of the world class technology the Navy possessed, the calibration pipe was merely a piece of pipe that was the same material and wall thickness of the discharge pipe, with duct tape taped to each end to hold the water/air that it contained. Really, we couldn't come up something more sophisticated than a piece of pipe and red neck chrome? She recalibrated the UT machine, or so she thought, and placed the pipe bag in the bag. She placed the sound powered radio back on her head and gave the "Thumbs Up" to the sailor standing on the deck of the sub. After an hour of watching the oscilloscope screen and relaying the information to the engine room, Lynn suddenly heard the radiation alarm. The HEPA filter had blown.

Standing next to Bill Turtle all Lynn could think of was, "The HEPA Filter had blown" as she looked at the totes of broken product in front of her.

Chapter 3

"The Lunch Bunch"

Bill Turtle escorted Lynn back to the entrance; all the while she apologized profusely for the error and assured him that ACME would do everything possible to correct the problem. She turned in her badge and walked to her Jeep under her umbrella. The rain was still pelting. She crawled in the driver's seat and just sat there for a minute, wondering if she should cry or scream. She did neither but backed her Jeep out of Hanscomb's Visitor Parking and turned toward the exit instead of letting her emotions get the best of her. It wasn't even 10:30 Am and she was already exhausted. The damn rain didn't help matters much either.

The ride back to ACME was uneventful, with Lynn catching herself obsessing over the issue with the thousands of bad parts and how she was going to break the news to Stan and Derek. She only caught snippets of songs on the radio and none of them were able to return Lynn to her daydream that she had on the ride out to Hanscomb's. She drove silently, deep in thought as she returned to the shop some 40 minutes later.

She pulled into her regular parking spot. It was the last space next to the building and near the back door. She preferred using the back door for a couple of reasons; 1.) It was closer to her office than the front door, and 2.) It gave her the opportunity to walk through the warehouse to see how the daily shipments were coming along. There had been a few more shipments added to the skid but not many. If shipments didn't pick up, ACME would be hard pressed to make goal this month. She thought, "Terrific, a major return and short sales". The hits just kept coming she mused. Lynn shook out her umbrella, the rain had been relentless during her trip and there was no sign of it letting up anytime soon. She made her way to her office and was relieved that the hallway stood empty, she really didn't think she was up to feeding the baby birds this morning. She nodded to Jake as she walked passed his desk on her way to her office, he piped, "Come tell me the bad news when you get settled." She retorted, "You really don't want to know."

Lynn booted up her computer and began the task of reviewing the 32 emails that came through during her absence. Dave Albert sent her a correspondence that the warehouse messed up another order for ACME's largest customer. Dave was a Project Manager and he handled the ICONIC account. This was his only job and because he managed the company's largest account he acted as if we were all there to do his bidding. She huffed and made a mental note to check on it with the warehouse but right now she had bigger fish to fry and Dave's complaint would be moved to number umpteenth and one down the hierarchy of "need to address now".

There was an email from Randy McDowell, the Supply Chain Manager, seeking assistance for the completion of a form for Conflict Minerals. This email moved up the food chain of "get it done." She perused the rest of her emails with a deftness of a speed reader, making mental notes as to priorities and what could just be slid over into the recycle bin.

She emerged from her office just in time to see Jake grab is car keys, she asked, "Where are you headed?"

He replied, "Its lunchtime in this gulag so I'm out to get something to eat, do you want anything?"

She thanked him for the offer as she remembered that she had brought her lunch with her that day. She checked her watch, grabbed her lunch bag and headed up front to have lunch with the gals. She was looking forward to it because she could use a laugh or two right about now. She was having a crappy day and it all started with the damn rain.

Lynn walked through the production facility with her bag of food and her water glass. She always drank ice water with her lunch and usually made one for the road when she left the front office kitchenette they ate in. She drank a lot of water and needed to in order to stay hydrated because when she rode her bike, she sweated profusely. Sometimes it embarrassed her with the amount of water that exuded from her body when she exercised, but this is the only time she wanted to perspire. Unless she was working out, perspiration bugged her, she didn't want to just sit and sweat, there had to be a reason for it unless she was sitting on the beach, then it was ok to sweat because everyone was covered with an oily sheen. She dropped her lunch bag at her customary position at the table. Sabina, one of the accountants always sat to her left and Jewel, the Finance Manager always sat directly across from her. Sabina and Lynn enjoyed working on the daily crossword puzzle and Jewel always stood at the ready with her phone in the event they got stuck. However, Sabina had strict crossword puzzle rules and words couldn't be looked up until all other efforts had been exhausted. Sabina worked crossword puzzles like balancing a ledger, everything had to add up. The girls entered the break room, went to their respective positions at the table, and for once today, everything seemed normal to Lynn

They jokingly bantered as they shared their lunches. The chicken wrap Lynn brought was cut into thirds, Jewel shared her carrot and celery sticks, Sabina brought some kind of pasta dish that neither Jewel nor herself was ready to partake so they politely excused themselves by saying that they had enough nourishment in front of them. They teased Lynn about Frank's boy school crush. She laughed back and said, "Hey, any attention is better than no attention." This opened the topic as to Lynn's love life or lack thereof. This was a subject that Lynn wasn't ready to discuss but went along with their questions and comments none-the-less. Jewel asked, "When are you going to start dating again Lynn?" She replied, "I wasn't aware that I had stopped dating." This made them think for a minute and was quickly followed up with, "So you are dating?"

Lynn stated, "No, all the good ones are taken, besides, I'm waiting for Ms. Right."

Everyone at work knew that Lynn was into women and not once did anyone ever make her feel uncomfortable. They never shamed her and always made her feel included. She felt very blessed to work in such an environment. Even Frank knew she was a lesbian and still loved her.

Sabina stated as a matter of fact, "If you don't go to clubs you'll never meet anyone."

Lynn replied, "There has to be another means to meet women that doesn't consist of an alcoholic breath whizzing, "You sure are pretty."

No thank you, the bar scene was out.

Jewel piped up from the other end of the table, "Why don't you try one of those dating apps?"

Lynn thought about it for a minute and rhetorically asked, "Don't you have to talk about yourself and list what you like and don't like?"

Jewel half stated, "Yes, is that a problem?"

Lynn vehemently replied, "Hell yes, that's a problem because I don't like talking about myself in person, let alone leaving my information out on the world wide web."

Jewel just shook her head and bit down on a carrot stick. Lynn noticed the head shake and asked, "What?" Jewel swallowed her chewed carrot and stated, "As long as you live alone in that cabin in the woods of yours, you will never meet anyone, you have to go out and get it. Or do you think Ms. Right is just going to walk up and knock on your door."

Lynn jokingly said, "It could happen."

"Oh yeah right", said Jewel, "With your luck it would be a Jehovah's Witness there to save your soul." If it wasn't so sad, Lynn would've agreed with her.

About this time Sabina offered up, "I'll write your profile for you, it'll be fun!"

Lynn raised her eyebrows in fear; there was no way she was going to let Sabina write her profile for a dating app that she had no intentions of using.

Sabina caught the look of terror on Lynn's face and quickly added, "I wouldn't post anything that you didn't want and you would have the final say on everything."

This brought little comfort to Lynn but it would give her some type of control over the information disseminated to the rest of the world or at least her local area. Lynn shook the thought from her head.

Sabina left the room and returned with a piece of paper, she shoved her crossword puzzle out of the way, turned to Lynn and said, "Ok, give it up."

Lynn looked at her incredulously and blatantly said, "Oh hell to the NO."

Jewel slightly choked on a celery stick and Lynn stated, "You deserved that!" Sabina just stared at Lynn, patiently waiting for her to tell her what to write.

Lynn looked back and said, "I don't know what to tell you."

Jewel immediately went to her phone and in a supportive voice, said, "I'll help!"

All of a sudden, Lynn's chicken wrap felt like a brick in the bottom of her stomach, there was no way of getting out of this interrogation now. She looked at the clock on the microwave and noticed that there was still twenty five minutes left of this agony.

Jewel tapped her phone and replied, "Oh my, there are hundreds of these apps." She listed off the top ten, with the first three being for straight people only. Those were immediately ignored as she announced, "Alternative Dating", "Date Now", "In No Time", and "See for Yourself".

Sabina quickly interjected, "Oh, pick "In No Time", I have a friend that had really good luck on that site."

Lynn asked, "How many gay friends do you have?"

Sabina said, "A few."

Both Jewel and Lynn looked at her inquisitively but decided not to broach the subject. Jewel went back to her phone and tapped on the website to register Lynn and develop her profile. Lynn could feel her anxiety level begin to build and dreaded the first question. Jewel asked her, her name.   Oh no, the pressure!

Jewel: First and Last Name

Lynn: Lynn Perry, why do I have to give my last name?

Jewel: You don't

Lynn: Then leave that part out

Jewel: Age

Lynn: 35

Jewel: Woman Seeking Woman

Lynn: Of Course

Jewel: Looking For?

Lynn: No One

Jewel: Not an option, get serious

Lynn: What are my choices?

Jewel: 1.) Friendship, 2.) Casual Friendship, 3.) Serious Relationship, 4.) Travel Partner, 5.) Pen Pal

Lynn: Number 1, number 4, and number 5

Jewel: Ok, Number 1, Number 3, and Number 4

Lynn: Wait a minute, definitely not number 3 and I really don't feel comfortable getting into a stranger's car so no to number 4 also.

Jewel: Be quiet

Sabina: I love to travel

Lynn: Be quiet

Jewel: Education

Lynn: Completed Pre-School

Jewel: Get serious, Education – Degree

Jewel: Religion

Lynn: Agnostic

Sabina: I didn't know you didn't believe in God.

Lynn: It's not that I don't, there is just no proof that God exists.

Jewel: Body Type

Lynn: Fat and miserable

Jewel: Lean and Trim

Jewel: Eye color, Blue

Jewel: Height

Lynn: 3'11"

Jewel: Come on, how tall are you?

Lynn: 5'4"

Jewel: Hair Color

Lynn: Orange

Jewel: Light Brown

Jewel: Occupation

Lynn: Freeloader

Jewel: (Rolled   her   eyes) Technical/Science/Computers/Engineering

Jewel: Income

Lynn: Poor as a church mouse

Jewel: No Answer

Lynn: Thank you, that's the first question you've answered correctly since we started this mess.

Jewel: Political affiliation

Lynn: Communist

Sabina: Are you really?

Lynn: Are you serious? I was in the Navy, a total patriot.

Jewel: No Answer

Lynn: Good on you, you correctly answered question number two

Jewel: Ethnicity

Lynn: Martian

Jewel: White/Caucasian

Jewel: Children

Lynn: Nine

Jewel: No kids

Jewel: Smoking preference

Lynn: Hookah Pipe

Jewel: Non Smoker

Lynn: Are we almost finished? I want to go back to work.

Sabina: We still have fifteen minutes before lunch is over

Jewel: We are almost finished

Jewel: Now there is a category for you to add things

Lynn: Add like what things?

Jewel: I don't know, it is like a Comments Section, it says, "Things I'd like to Add"

Lynn: I like to add numbers

Sabina: I don't think that is what they mean.

Lynn: Ok, how about, "I love to work on my house and building furniture is my best therapy so if you're ok with a little saw dust, we'll be great."

Jewel: Do you really have to talk about saw dust? It makes you sound Butch and you're more femme than butch.

Lynn: But it's the truth

Jewel: Ok, I'll leave it but the whole point of this exercise is to get you a date, not to alienate you from the female species

Jewel: Next section, "The one I'm looking for."

Lynn: A rich widow that has one foot in the grave and the other on a banana peeling.

Jewel: If you don't take this serious, I'm just going to fill in the blanks for you.

Lynn: Oh ok, ok. Let me see, how about, "I'm looking for a down to earth person who enjoys life and going on adventures. An outdoor lover is a must and finds that taking a long car ride is the easiest way to get to know someone.

Sabina: Oh that's good, I like that.

Jewel: Do you really think that going on a long car ride is the easiest way to get to know someone?

Lynn: Yes, there is nowhere to go unless you jump out of moving vehicle so you have nothing to do but look at the scenery and talk.

Jewel: That actually makes sense

Jewel: Ok, next category, "In a Nutshell"

Lynn: Oh I don't know; nuts?

Sabina: I think they want a summary of you.

Lynn: What? Like Cliff's Notes?

Jewel: Yes, you geek!

Lynn: Ok, write this, "I'm honest, loyal, and have integrity. I always keep my word. The greatest gift you can give someone is a smile; it's a good ice breaker, so smile even if it's just for yourself."

Sabina: Oh another good one! You're a natural at this.

Lynn: That's it, I'm done.

Jewel: But we're not finished. There are still Personality Questions, Interests and Hobbies, Message Ideas. You can't leave yet.

Lynn: Oh yes I can, I'm outta here.

And with that, Lynn cleaned up her area, grabbed her lunch bag, re-filled her ice water and left the break room.

Jewel yelled, "We're going to finish this for you!"

Lynn yelled back, "Do what you will!"

She left the front offices and walked through Production to get back to her office, shaking her head and thinking to herself, "That was grueling; I haven't answered that many questions since I enlisted in the Navy." Without another thought about it, Lynn began her mental checklist for afternoon work.

Jewel and Sabina worked vigorously to complete her profile as Lynn made her way back to her work spaces. They added her personality traits to the mix.

Q: Do you enjoy cooking

A: I love it

Q: How patient do you consider yourself

A: Extremely patient

Q: Are you romantic

A: Very romantic

Q: How punctual are you typically

A: Always on time

Q: Do you enjoy going to the movies

A: Love it

Q: How much do you enjoy going to live theater?

A: There's nothing better

Q: How much do you like reading?

A: I love it

     They added what they thought Lynn's Interests and Hobbies would be.

Fitness

"I love my bike"

Books and Reading

"A rainy day with a book, a cup of coffee, and a great conversation is the best."

Nature and Outdoors

"We have a great planet, let's enjoy it."

Quite pleased with what they accomplished, they looked at each and giggled. Sabina said, "Oh she is so much going to get a date!" They both finished cleaning up the break room and went back to work with smiles of satisfaction on their faces.

Unaware of the speed and desperation of the internet, Lynn remained clueless as to the inner workings of servers and what was happening behind the scenes of the dating website she just joined. Instant messages, matches, and meetings were occurring with break neck speed, yet Lynn was oblivious until she would get home that night and find a myriad of contacts and emails from "Our Time".

Chapter 4

"In No Time"

Lynn found herself standing in her office, shaking her head at the thought fo Jewel and Sabina completing her profile for the dating site, she pondered the possibilities, but doubted that anything would come of it. She sat down and busied herself with the work that she had planned to do that afternoon but remembered that she needed to generate a corrective action and an RMA (Return Material Authorization) so that Bill Turtle could send the bad product back to ACME. It took all of the energy she had to type in twenty-seven thousand in the quantity block of the database. Never had she had such a large return here at ACME or anywhere else she had worked. Things like this just didn't happen to her. She prided herself in being a good Quality Manager and had handpicked the crew that she was currently working with, and they were spot on most of the time. This time, not so much!

Jake stepped into Lynn's office and asked, "Well, how bad is it?"

Lynn didn't even look up from her data entry into the Nonconformance Database and said, "Bad, it's really bad. At $3.50 a pop, we're looking at a customer credit of what?"

Lynn waited for Jake to do the mental math and he summed up with, "Almost a hundred grand!"

Lynn clenched her jaw to the point of pain, and nodded, "You're about right with your summation."

In a low voice, Jake said, "Stan and Derek are going to have a meltdown. I've been here almost twenty years and I can't remember a return this large."

Lynn tore her eyes away from her monitor and looked at Jake. All she could think to say was "Really?"

He looked at her and with the innocence of a child said, "What? What did I say?"

Lynn peered at him through squinted eyes and said, "Dammit Jake, I could've gone a lifetime without hearing that this has been the largest return in twenty years."

Realizing what he had said he quickly offered up, "But it will be ok, you got this. Stan and Derek may be a little miffed, but they will get over it. They have a lot of respect for you and they know that you will do your best to make this right. You always have."

She let Jake's compliment cover her like a warm blanket. She needed to hear it and was a little perturbed at herself for snapping at Jake the way she did and was really upset that she used profanity to express her anger. This wasn't like her; she had worked really hard to clean up her language after being in the Navy. It's true what they mean when they say, "She cussed like a sailor."

Lynn got up from her desk, made the tight squeeze between Jake and the doorframe, and made a beeline for the coffee pot. She needed a cup of Joe if she was going to make it through this afternoon. She looked up at the clock and the hour hand was on two, she thought, *"Good, I can make it through another two hours."*

Jake was watching her from the doorway and half asked, "Are you sure you should be drinking that? You're wound tighter than an eight-day clock right now."

Lynn just looked at him and had no comeback. She knew he was right, but she was low on her daily intake of caffeine and was starting to get a headache. At least that is what she told herself, the headache could be coming on from pure stress at this point. Lynn returned to her desk, squeezing by Jake again only this time holding a scalding hot cup of coffee. She made sure not to spill it and Jake didn't seem like he was going to be moving anytime soon.

Lynn thought that the best way to get Jake out of her office was to give a task so she said, "I need you to go to the warehouse and pull any and all of these parts out of inventory so we make sure they don't get shipped to Hanscomb's by mistake."

With a little salute and an "Aye Aye Captain," Jake left to go to the warehouse. Lynn swiveled back to her desk and finished up the data entry, all the while sipping on her coffee, and formulating what she was going to tell Stan and Derek.

Lynn finished her liquid courage and set off to find Stan and Derek. She found them both in Stan's office going over the latest work schedules. They were contemplating going to a 4x10 work schedule in production in hopes that they would have more machine uptime and improve efficiency for needed future capacity. They both looked up when Lynn tapped on the door.

Stan said, "Oh come in Lynn, we want to get your opinion on these new work schedules." Stan briefly explained the concept and Lynn liked it they just didn't know what to do with the second shift.

"Second shift should be just fine, they are already working four ten-hour days," Lynn offered.

Stan and Derek looked at each other and Stan nodded his head toward Lynn and said, "That's why I hired her."

Lynn half-jokingly said, "You might want to rethink that after I tell you about my trip to Hanscomb's."

Stan looked at her worriedly and stated, "It's pretty bad over there isn't it?"

Lynn nodded her head up and down.

At which time Derek yelled, "Damn it to hell!"

Neither Lynn nor Stan reacted to this outburst because it was common for Derek to express his feelings in such a colorful manner. Lynn perceived this outburst from Derek to give Stan the impression that he cared about what was going on over at Hanscomb's. Which Lynn thought that Derek did care, but she also knew that he wouldn't do anything about it, even when the product came back to be reworked. Derek wanted to make sure that Stan perceived this problem as a "Quality" issue which took the owness off him for his group making bad product. Production could make bad product all day long but if the QC Inspectors missed one nonconforming part then suddenly, the blame shifted to the Quality group and off of the Production group. This always aggravated Lynn throughout her entire career but she had grown accustomed to being the whipping post for Operations. Even though this was not true in all aspects, it was her reality at work.

Lynn briefly explained the problem with the defective parts and stated that she had determined the root cause to be the "continuation" process that was used in Production for long running parts. The current process required a First Piece Inspection prior to running any job in order to ensure the machine was set up properly and was making good parts before an order for thousands of parts commenced. Typically, this was an effective process and prevented scrap from being made. However, with a "continuation", the job could essentially keep running for days without any inspection being performed by Quality Control. If anything went wrong with the machine and the part, it would virtually go undetected and make its way to the warehouse and to the customer without notice. Derek continued to re-direct blame on the Quality group by stating, "So much for in-process inspection." This angered Lynn because the parts were made in Production and they are required to inspect the parts every hour, but this didn't seem to register with Derek.

Stan sat there looking at Lynn and waited for her response to Derek's accusation. For the sake of argument, Lynn bit her tongue and decided not to express her thoughts on the matter. She had enough problems without creating more with verbal onslaughts at Derek.

Stan gave her a reassuring look that said, "I know the real deal, no worries."

Lynn nodded and silently mouthed, "Thank you."

Stan tipped is head in return and Derek sat there oblivious to the interaction that had transpired between the two of them.

He just kept spouting condescension like, "Why do we even have a QC Department if they're not going to catch our mistakes?"

That was it, Lynn couldn't keep it in any longer and her ire boiled to the surface. She shot an angry look at Derek and opened her mouth to speak but before she could say anything, Stan interjected, "Let's all try to focus on the positive. Yes, the credit is going to be a big hit to our finances this month but we are having a great month in shipments even if sales are down so we will be able to weather the monetary storm that's going to hit us at the end of the month." He turned to Derek and asked, "How do you plan on reworking Production's mistake?"

Derek frowned and was somewhat perturbed that Stan chose to chastise him in front of Lynn.

Derek replied, "I don't know yet, I'll have to get with Engineering and develop a machine program that will correct the defect without damaging the part."

Stan said, "Good, why don't you get on that." then he turned to Lynn and said, "Thank you for dropping everything this morning and going over there. It meant a lot to me and to Hanscomb."

Lynn nodded, "Of course, anything for the team." Silently seething and with a flushed face, Derek rose from his chair and left Stan's office. Stan and Lynn looked at each other and he could tell by the look on his face that she was not happy with how the encounter with Derek had ended.

Stan smiled reassuringly and said, "Don't worry about him, he'll get over it until some other department makes a mistake then he will point his accusatory finger at them."

Lynn looked at Stan and said, "Yeah, but why does he have to be right? We should've caught that mistake in QC but we dropped the ball."

With a concerned look on his face, Stan offered, "Lynn, you can't catch everything." Lynn tried to agree with him but in the depths of her soul, she so much felt like she had failed.

With a heavy heart, Lynn left Stan's office and walked slowly back to her office. It was now late in the evening and most of the office doors in the hallway were closed, indicating that everyone had gone home for the evening. Not to be knocked down too far, Lynn straightened her shoulders, and with chin up, walked quietly down the hall way.

She shook her head when she got back to her office and saw all of the work that she didn't accomplish that day and said, "Oh to hell with it, I'm going home."

She powered down her computer, grabbed her purse and umbrella, turned off the light, and shut the door. When she was leaving the building, she noticed that the rain had finally stopped, she said a small prayer of gratitude, and walked to her Jeep. She turned the ignition and the engine turned over and started. Lynn backed out of her spot and drove to the exit of the parking lot. The short ride home seemed interminable as she sat in silence, not wanting to hear the radio or any other noise for that matter.

Lynn drove the Jeep up her steep gravel driveway, bumping and bouncing all the way, and reminded herself to contact the landscapers to come out and grade it for her. The winter snow and spring rains had wreaked havoc on her driveway, and it had turned into a kidney buster with deep ruts and potholes. This was just one more annoyance in a day full of annoyances. She pulled her purse over the passenger seat, picked up her umbrella, and climbed out the Jeep. As she unlocked her back door, she noted that she needed to sweep off the leaves off of the deck before they stained the stain. Lynn considered the pun humorous and walked into her cabin in the woods. She loved her home, especially when it was snowing, and she had the wood stove cranked up. The Great Room was always cozy and inviting regardless of snow or no snow. She was always glad to be home after a hard day at work. The cabin seemed to wrap her in its wooden arms and let her know that everything was going to be ok. She hung her purse on the hook, along with her car keys, and went to the kitchen to turn on the stove top to boil water for a cup of tea. Without hesitation, she turned to her left, went into the bathroom and turned on the shower. She needed to cleanse this day away. Forgetting about the boiling tea kettle, she stripped herself of her clothes and stepped into the shower of hot water and put her head directly under the shower head. She closed her eyes and let the water pour over her hair, down her face, and along her shoulders. She put a quarter size dollop of shampoo in her palm and began to vigorously wash her hair; it felt good to scratch her scalp with her fingers. It made her head tingle. Lynn rinsed her hair and picked up her sponge to perform the same action on her body. Satisfied that the day's grime was gone, she quickly rinsed, turned off the water, and pulled her towel from the hook. As soon as the water slowed to a drip, Lynn could hear the tea kettle whistling from the kitchen.

She quickly toweled off, put on a pair of baggy running shorts and her one of her favorite tee shirts. She loved her white v-neck tee shirts;

she had ten of them that she carefully folded after doing laundry and placed in her chest of drawers. She donned a pair of white booties and her slippers and darted to the kitchen to turn off the stove top. The tea pot slowed down its whistle until it was just a sputter. She took a mug out of the cabinet and placed a tea bag of Earl Grey into the cup and poured the hot steaming water over it. She took her tea and sat down at her desk to check her personal emails. She booted up her brain and opened her Yahoo account and said aloud to no one, "What fresh hell is this?"

She looked at the counter and it read that she had received twenty-one emails and seven of them were from the dating website, "In No Time". Under her breath, she cursed Sabina and Jewel for going through with developing her profile. She opened the earliest one received, and it thanked her for registering and to 'get ready to find love.' Oh great, this is going to be a debacle, she clicked on the delete button. The second email told her that in order to experience the 'full effect' of the website, she could 'Boost' her profile for the bargain rate of twenty dollars; this is fifty percent off the going rate if she acted now. *No thank you, delete*. The third email was instructions as to how to use the site and what each of the buttons and categories meant. She quickly read through the 'how to make contact' category and deleted this email as well. When she opened the fourth email, it told her that Maryellen had 'liked' her profile and left a little note saying, 'great picture'. She didn't remember anything about a picture when she was in the break room with Jewel and Sabina.

She quickly clicked on 'Your Profile' and looked at the picture the two crazy women had posted. She remembered the photo from last year's Christmas Party, and it was of Lynn helping herself to a glass of Sprite. She had to admit, they had picked out a decent picture of her, even though she was wearing an ugly Christmas Sweater. Regardless of what she was wearing, it was a good picture of her face. Her blue eyes sparkled, her teeth a brilliant white against her tanned skin. She silently thanked the tanning bed at the gym. Her dimples were deep and her cheeks rosy. Yes, she was pleased with the photo. She noticed that there were three other pictures posted as well. *Oh no, what now?!?* She clicked on one and it opened with her standing in front of her Jeep. She remembered this one as well. Jewel had taken it when Lynn first bought her Jeep to capture the moment when she would begin making the car payments. Every month on the day the payment was due, Jewel sent her the pic and said, only 'blank' number of payments left. Lynn just thought it was an accounting thing they obsessed about and just shook her head every month when she opened the routine email. The second picture was of the three of them at the company picnic. Another good picture of Lynn but Jewel was a little flushed in the face from one too many cups of beer from the party keg. The last picture was of Lynn at her desk in deep concentration. She didn't remember this picture being taken and made a mental note to ask both Jewel and Sabina when she got to work tomorrow. All in all, they did a good job in the picture department. She deleted Maryellen's email.

The fifth email was from someone named Shay. The website said that Shay was in Brooklyn, NY and this caused Lynn to pause and think, "What? There are no women in Brooklyn?" Shay had left her phone number and said, "Text me, I would like to get to know you." Not knowing any better, Lynn plugged in her phone number and hit the 'Send' button. Later she thought about it and told herself that that was stupid because she didn't even know this woman. She justified her mistake by telling herself that she wasn't familiar with the workings of the website, plus she could block her if she turned out to be a psycho. She deleted this email also. Lynn opened the sixth email and quickly deleted it, whoever that woman was needed a dentist in a bad way. The seventh and final email was from a woman named Gram from a town in Vermont. Lynn studied the picture of the woman and found her appearance to be pleasant and she had a nice smile, but in both pictures, the woman was wearing sunglasses so Lynn couldn't see if her smile touched her eyes but she thought that it probably did. Her profile read that she was Lynn's age, degreed, stood 5'0", worked in marketing, and had brown eyes. Lynn noted that this woman saw a dentist on a regular basis because she had gorgeous teeth. Oral hygiene was particularly important to Lynn. Lynn saw that Gram had given her a 'Thumbs Up' and she perceived that to be a good sign on this website. Lynn thought to herself, *"Maybe there is something to this online dating thing after all."* Lynn clicked on the little envelope icon to send a return message. She thanked Gram for the 'thumbs up' and was hoping that they could connect in the future. To be considerate, Lynn typed, "Have a wonderful day!" She saved this email.

Lynn finished reading her other thirteen emails. One was from her brother and sister-in-law, they had sent the latest pictures of her nephews and she noticed that they were growing like weeds; she jotted a note on the tablet next to her pc that said, "Make travel plans to see Chris." There were three emails that should've went to Spam, so she went in and increased the filter to block ads for erectile dysfunction. She also deleted emails from Dominos Pizza and Anderson Windows. Domino's didn't deliver to her neck of the woods and she was not currently in need of any windows. Having cleaned out her mailbox, Lynn powered down her computer and reached up and snapped of the table lamp on her desk. Her tea had gotten cold, she had forgotten all about it. She took her cup to the kitchen, tossed the tea bag in the sink, and dumped the cold tea into the sink. She rinsed her cup and placed it in the strainer.

Lynn went in the bathroom to perform her nightly ritual of brushing her teeth and rubbing her moisturizer into her face. As she brushed her teeth, her mind returned to the picture of Gram. Even though she didn't spend a lot of time studying the picture, her mind's eye seemed to have been able to capture every detail of the woman's face. Gram had the beginnings of slight crow's feet around her eyes which meant that she smiled a lot and this pleased Lynn. She too liked to smile and then she looked at her own image in the mirror to examine the wrinkles on her face. She too was beginning to see her puppet lines and slight indents from her dimples. Gram had seven pictures posted on her profile and one of the pictures was of her and an elderly woman, probably her grandmother or possibly an aunt. This gave Lynn the impression that she could possibly be kind and thoughtful. In her "In a Nut Shell" caption she had written, "I am doing my best to live a happy and peaceful life. Trying to do so with no regrets. Having a warm hug at the end of the day is pure joy!!" Lynn liked this. In every picture of Gram, she is smiling so Lynn deduced that she is living a happy life just as she had written. Lynn finished her nightly regime, put her toothbrush in the holder, rinsed her mouth and went into her bedroom. She turned down the covers, climbed in, reached up and turned off her bedside lamp, and shut her eyes as her mind continued to see Gram's face. Maybe, just maybe, this could be a good thing.

Chapter 5

"Annie"

As she sat on the barstool at the kitchen counter in her condo, Annie pushed her horn rimmed glasses back up her nose and picked up the next essay to grade. Even though her class had too many students, the parent teacher conferences were sparsely attended, and the syllabus was taxing, she loved teaching. Her greatest joy was when she could see the light bulbs come on their faces and her kids "Got It". She had a good group this year and it was semesters like this that made it all worthwhile. Teaching could be a thankless job and dealing with angry parents because she gave their child a "D" on a paper could almost make a nun scream, but Annie persevered and did her best to help that same student raise their grade to a "C" on the next paper. She couldn't remember a time when she didn't want to teach and it was somewhat in her DNA. Her Aunt Mary was a teacher and she bestowed in Annie a foundation of learning, ever being consistent and encouraging her to pursue that which she was designed for; molding the young minds of the future. She crinkled her nose as she read the paper that she held in her hand and thought, "I know this student, they can do better." She picked up her red pen and began circling misspellings, placing commas where they belonged, and wrote "run on sentence" in the margin of a paragraph that contained no punctuation other than the last period. She thought about the student who wrote the essay and knew that his home life wasn't the greatest, this, coupled with the knowledge that some kids were punished for bad grades; she put a big red "B" at the top of the paper even though it was only worthy of a "C". Annie murmured to herself, "I promise to be a better teacher for you."

Needing to stretch, Annie got up and walked over to the sliding doors that led to the balcony of her condo. She pulled back the vertical blinds and squinted at the bright New Mexico sun streaming though the panes. She felt the door glass and it was warm. It was only 9:00 in the morning and she could tell that it was going to be another hot day in Albuquerque. The Land of Enchantment was quickly turning into the Land of Hell Hot and she thought it best to spend the day indoors in the air conditioning grading papers rather than go to the store to get what little groceries she needed. It was still Saturday and she could wait to go to the store tomorrow to pick up anything she might need to get her through the next week. She walked over to the area between her dining room and living room, stopped, bent at the waist, and placed her flat palms on the carpeted floor, her blonde hair falling in front of her shoulders. It felt good to stretch and her spine cracked and popped as it released the pressure from her lower back. She had been grading papers since 7:00 that morning while having her morning coffee and hadn't moved until now. She made a mental note, "Take more breaks." She walked her hands out in front of her until her body created an inverted "V" and was glad that her body remained limber and nimble in spite of not being able to get to dance class as often as she liked.

If teaching was her first passion, dancing was her second, followed by music. Annie couldn't remember if she liked dancing before she liked music but thought that she probably wouldn't dance without music so she mentally changed the passion line up and put music before dancing. She pushed herself up to a standing position and did a quick pirouette. She had a dancer's body, lean and toned, with shapely legs, a flat stomach, and a tight butt. She was actually a very pretty girl with long hair, hazel eyes, and a small pointed nose. However, her humility wouldn't let her think such things. She knew that she was healthy and took great pride in trying to keep her body in good physical well being. In fact, she was seriously contemplating becoming vegan because she heard it was the best thing a person could do for their body. She hadn't made the complete u-turn from meat because she still had a weakness for Cajun chicken with pasta, a dish she absolutely craved two to three times a month but only indulged once every four weeks. She loved it so much that she even had it penciled in on the calendar that hung on her fridge, "Red Lobster-Cajun Chicken with Pasta".

Thinking she could listen to music while she completed grading papers, she walked over and turned on her Bose Wave Radio/CD player. It was one of the few extravagances she allowed herself; her condo was sparsely furnished with a few of the pieces being second hand and picked up at garage sales and thrift stores. She didn't mind and really placed no importance on material things. Not many people came to visit except for family and she didn't feel the need to impress family. Her money was used for the necessities in life like a roof over her head, a vehicle to drive, and food to eat. Most of her extra money went to support her passions often spending her own finances to buy needed school supplies that were not provided by the district, pay for her dance classes, and buy a new CD when she heard a tune on the radio that she just couldn't live without, and of course her wifi. She surfed the net on a daily basis keeping her tethered to the outside world and informed on current events. She felt the need to stay up on the happenings that interested her students so that she could effectively communicate with them on their level. She watched YouTube on a regular basis, usually catching the latest Dance Convention, one of her favorites was the Budafest Convention held in California every year. She marveled at the dancers and how well they performed waltzes and Salsa, but her favorite was West Coast Swing and a person just couldn't be in a bad mood when dancing to such an upbeat positive tempo. Although she would love to just push the papers aside and dance, she placed some of her slower melodies in her Bose, readjusted her shorts and tee shirt, and went back to grading papers.

Around noon, and two dozen essays later, she felt the first rumblings of hunger and chuckled to herself for not heeding her own advice for "Take more breaks". She pulled a yogurt, some grapes, and a bottle of water from the fridge and sat down at her dining room table to partake in her little brunch for one. Although used to being alone, there were times when she thought how pleasant it would be to be sharing her yogurt and grapes with another woman that shared her interests and passions in life. She could see her imaginary lover sitting across the table from her popping grapes into her mouth and just chit chatting about what they were going to do that afternoon. Maybe they could go for a ride in the desert, or catch a matinee, or go shopping in Old Town or Nob Hill. It didn't matter what they did, as long as they were together, walking through the open market arm in arm, trying on silly hats, waddling like penguins, sharing an apple purchased from a local grower. It was these simple pleasures that meant the most to Annie. She knew there was someone out there for her but where, she did not know. She blinked back the tears that had formed in her eyes and swallowed the lump in her throat. She put the grapes back in the fridge, tossed the yogurt container in the trash, wiped off the table, and resumed her seat at the kitchen counter.

Try as she might, she just couldn't read one more essay written by another 5th grader, she needed to do something else. All of a sudden, her spacious condo seemed too small and she needed to get out for awhile. Barefooted, she walked into her bedroom, pulled out her running shorts, ankle socks, and sports bra from the chest of drawers, grabbed a tee shirt from the closet and in two shakes she was ready to go for a run. She slipped into her running shoes, went to the bathroom to switch out her glasses with her contacts, and headed for the front door. She slipped her driver's license into the pocket of her shorts, unhooked her spare key from the hook by the door, and put it in the other pocket. She opened the door of her condo and was immediately met with a blast from the furnace of the New Mexico heat. She silently cursed and almost had second thoughts about the run, but she knew that afterward, she would've sweated the unrealistic daydreams from her head as well as the toxins from her body.

She walked out to the courtyard and began stretching her legs in preparation of her run. She put one foot up on a bench and bent forward, putting her forehead on her kneecap and touching her toes with her fingers. The sun warmed her body and helped stretch out her hamstrings and calves. She shifted her feet and stretched out her other hamstring; her long body resembling a straight line between the ground and the bench. Satisfied with the feeling, she changed positions and bending at the knee, lifted her leg behind her a stretched out her quad and shin muscles. She stood on her other foot and stretched out the other leg. All she had done was stretch and she was already sweating buckets but she noted that her mind was beginning to clear. She ran in place and shook out her hands and started her run. She ran, her feet pounding the pavement, and the sweat began to pour. She was about a mile into her three mile run when she fell into her "zone". Her "zone" being that place where her mind is thinking of nothing and all she can hear is her heart beating with her breath as she deeply inhaled and exhaled. At least she wasn't thinking; her goal achieved. Annie had no thoughts of another woman, or of 5th grade essays, or of what she needed to pick up at the market. She just ran, and ran, and ran.

Annie rounded the last corner back to her condo and started to slow down her pace. She had slowed to a walk by the time she entered her courtyard. She put her hands on her hips and continued to walk around the fountain that was the centerpiece of her condo complex. Her entire body was covered with perspiration. Her tee shirt was soaked through as was her shorts. She knew that the shower would be so worth it. She continued to walk as her breathing returned to normal and made her way to her condo door. She unlocked the door and just as much as the heat hit her on her way out, the coolness of the AC hit her when she walked back in. Annie immediately felt a chill rush through her body, the sweat on her body felt like it had turned to ice, and her shirt and shorts became blankets of snow. She quickly re-hooked her spare house key and dropped her ID on the counter. She turned and locked her door and raced to the bathroom to start her shower. It only took a few minutes to get the water temperature warm. She quickly shed her clothes, pulled back the shower curtain, and stepped into the spray of warmth that began to cover her body. This was the best part of her run, the getting clean part. She reached up, grabbed her loofa, and squeezed body wash along its length. She scrubbed as if she was prepping for surgery and her skin began to tingle. The white soap suds were a stark contrast to her tanned body. She let the water beat her back, loosening the tight but well formed muscles. She turned around, faced the shower head, put her hands against the wall, and let the water pelt her scalp. She started breathing out of her mouth, blowing the water away as if she was coming up from a deep swim. With her eyes closed, she reached up to the caddy and found her shampoo. She squeezed a generous amount into her palm and began to wash her long locks of hair. She had beautiful hair and it was one of her better physical attributes; everyone commented on her hair. It was blonde with streaks of honey blonde mixed in giving her a look of natural highlights. Most women pay hundreds of dollars for hair that looked like Annie's, but for her, it came naturally. She was born with it and couldn't understand what the big deal was when other women, and even men, complimented on her hair.

Just like the water running over her, Annie let her mind run away to a place in which there as a woman standing behind her in the shower, her body pressed against her, as the woman gently washed Annie's hair. So much for the 3 mile run cleansing her thoughts of unrealistic images of a loving partner to share her life with, but at least her body was clean. She reached down and turned the shower off. She was frustrated and mad at herself for not being able to rid her brain of the images that caused her heart pain. "Just face it Annie, you're lonely", she thought. She reached behind the shower curtain, found her towel hanging on the hook and began to dry her body, wiping the water away. Too bad she couldn't wipe away the thoughts that arrested her mind and held her emotions hostage.

Chapter 6

"The Market"

      Annie finished grading the papers on Sunday, along with going to the market and doing laundry. Her Sunday proved to be uneventful with the exception of going to the market to shop for groceries, but even that little trip went without any surprises. Unless you want to count the run in with an old friend that she had at the market. She followed her same routine, starting in dairy and ending in produce. In the dairy aisle she put two 4 packs of Greek Yogurt in her cart, this would last her throughout the week and next weekend when she went to the market again. Her life and become so routine that she didn't even have to think about it anymore. Annie often pondered, "Am I just existing?" She added some whipped cream cheese to her basket with a mental note to pick up some bagels; she was in the mood for a bagel with cream cheese. She didn't know if she wanted to get some smoked salmon or capers to go with her bagel. She would decide when she looked at the prices. She pointed her cart to the bread aisle and as she was pushing her cart she saw a woman that looked familiar. As she got closer, she did recognize the woman as a friend of hers when she was in past relationship. The woman had been a friend when Annie was a couple with Lisa. It had been two years since her last relationship and was in no hurry to jump back into anything soon. Her relationship had ended badly with Lisa and some of the scars had not quite healed yet.

Annie quickly thought about ducking into another aisle to avoid the woman but it was too late, she could see her waving in the distance. Margaret was an ok friend but she was closer to Lisa than Annie and Annie considered her more of an acquaintance than an actual friend. After the breakup, the mutual friends that they had together chose sides and Lisa retained most of the women on her side. Annie didn't mind, she had a short tolerance for rude and self-centered people and the majority of the people that they hung out with were just that, she only tolerated them for Lisa. Even though some of the scars had not healed, because when Annie loves, she loves deeply and with a mindset that she is in for the long haul. Now that she thought about it, Lisa belonged with the group of friends that had left Annie high and dry. Lisa could be quite selfish at times. Like when Annie's car was in the shop and she needed a ride to work, all of a sudden it was a major inconvenience for Lisa. Even though they worked the same hours, Lisa couldn't drive the 3 miles out of her way to drop Lisa off at school. Having thought this, Annie knew that she had made the right decision. Oh no, here comes Margaret!

Annie put on her best smile as Margaret approached her but Margaret would have none of that, she quickly left her buggy in the middle of the aisle and approached Annie with arms extended. Annie thought, *Oh no, here comes a hug*. Margaret engulfed Annie in a bear hug and Annie could not escape. Margaret was a large woman, not massive, but tall and thick. Her presence was known immediately whenever she entered a room. Annie was slender, stood 5'6" and weighed in around 125. Margaret was twice as big as Annie and Annie could hear her back pop when Margaret hugged her.

As soon as she felt Margaret loosen her death grip, Annie backed up and pleasantly said, "Hi Margaret, it's good to see you again."

Margaret wasted no time in regurgitating the past and in a loud voice said, "My Gosh Annie, no one has seen you since you and Lisa broke up."

Annie thought about stating that everyone they knew went to the dark side after the break up but decided not to, she just merely stated, "Oh, I've been around, busy at work, and what not." Annie inquired, "So how have you been? Are you still with Amy?"

Margaret jokingly replied, "Oh yes, we're going to die together. We had a Commitment Ceremony a year ago, didn't you get an invitation?" Annie shook her head, knowing full well that her name never made it to the invite list.

Margaret went on to tell Annie about the ceremony and how Lisa and Debbie stood up as witnesses.

She noticed the frown on Annie's face and rhetorically said, "Oh, you didn't know? Debbie and Lisa got together shortly after her break up with you."

Annie knew that Margaret knew the whole story so being coy with her put Annie on guard. Margaret didn't wait for a response from Annie and commenced to tell her how happy Lisa and Debbie were and that they were like an old married couple.

Margaret raised her eyebrows and said, "Yeah, they are fat and happy, if you know what I mean?" Annie was silently hoping that Margaret would remember that she left her cart behind and would go to get, which would give Annie a chance to flee, but no such luck. The cart still sat untouched, some twenty feet away from them.

Margaret continued, "Oh yes, they have both gained weight and you can tell that their relationship is going good, if you know what I mean?"

Annie could care less and thought, "If she says, 'you know what I mean' one more time I may have a fit of Tourette's syndrome and just start saying a string of profanities." However, Annie had class and wouldn't allow herself to stoop to such a level.

Margaret suddenly noticed Annie was standing there and said, "Well, you look great honey, are you still dancing? Your legs sure look like you are still dancing, they are hot, if you know what I mean?"

That was it, Annie went inside her brain and a litany of curse words began to formulate and make their way to her tongue, but before any words came out, Margaret rushed on with the summary of what had happened over the last two years.

Margaret asked, "Are you seeing anyone special?"

Annie sighed, more out of weariness than loss, and said, "No, I'm still single and there is no one special that I'm dating." She proffered, "I'm really busy with this year's class and I haven't had the time to think about a social life."

Margaret responded with, "Oh really, you know that Andrea is single now? She and Melody broke up about the same time as you and Lisa. You should give her a call and ask her to go out. I'm sure that she would love to hear from you. She always had a secret crush on you, if you know what I mean?"

Annie dismissed Margaret's announcement and silently seethed inside. Margaret said this on purpose because Margaret knew that that cause of the breakup between Annie and Lisa was due to the fact that Lisa had had an affair with Andrea.

Annie had had enough public persecution to last her a life time so she looked at her watch and exclaimed, "Oh my, look at the time, I need to finish up and get going."

Margaret eyed her warily and said, "But we just started talking!"

Annie apologized and rushed on to say that she had a mountain of papers to finish grading and that laundry was waiting.

Margaret said, "Ok, but there for a minute I thought you were trying to get rid of me."

"Oh no, it's just that I have a lot more to do today and then it's back to school on Monday. I need to scoot along," Annie replied.

"Yeah I get it. Hey? Do you want me to pass your number on to Andrea so she can give you a call?" Margaret asked.

Annie couldn't help it. She incredulously replied, "Now Margaret, you know that wouldn't be appropriate."

They both said their goodbyes and Margaret promised to stay in touch and Annie thought, *Oh please don't*.

Margaret bounded back to her cart and passed Annie on her way down the aisle; she put her hand on Annie's arm and in a serious voice said, "You know, Lisa really did love you." Margaret made her way down the aisle.

Annie just stood there dumbfounded and thought, *Did that really just happen? The audacity of some people never ceases to amaze me*. It took a minute for Annie to regain her composure and remember where she was. *Oh yes, in the market, needing bagels, capers, fruit, and vegetables*. Annie began to push her cart toward the condiment aisle. She quickly located her favorite brand of capers and placed them gently in her buggy. Her head was still reeling from the conversation with Margaret. Annie's thoughts were scattered and she kept having to remind herself as to why she was in this market pushing a cart. *Oh yes, bagels*. She entered the bread aisle and she didn't know whether to be sad or mad so she finally declared that she was both sad and mad. Sad because she was happy with Lisa and had no clue that there was a problem in the relationship. They got along splendidly (well at least when Lisa was in a giving mood), their sex life was fine, and they split the living expenses and the chores. Annie was completely shocked when Lisa walked in one day and said, "This isn't working for me anymore and I want out."

Annie was unloading the dishwasher when Lisa unloaded on her. She didn't even ask Annie to sit down. Annie was putting glasses in the cupboard when Lisa made her announcement and then she stood up and said, "Well, I guess I should go pack."

Annie thought maybe she didn't hear Lisa correctly and placed the glass in the cabinet, turn to Lisa and asked, "What did you say?"

Lisa repeated that the relationship wasn't working for her and wanted out.

"Yeah", Annie said, "I thought that's what you said." The dishes could wait and Annie followed Lisa into the bedroom, "What do you mean you want out?"

Lisa responded, "Just what I said. I'm done. It's time for me to move on."

Annie sat down on the bed and began to ask the questions that every person asks during a break up, "Was it me? What did I do? Why are you unhappy? Isn't there something we can do? Where are you going to go? What about us?" The list went on ad infinitum; *more like ad inauseoum* Annie thought to herself. She still remembers how she begged for answers and became quite annoyed with herself for begging. She thought better of herself than that and still can't believe that she asked Lisa to stay and work it out. It wasn't until after the break up that Annie learned that Lisa was having an affair with Andrea. She had always thought highly of Andrea and considered her one of the better ones that they hung out with on a regular basis.

Annie finally made it to the produce department and began selecting her fruits and vegetables. She picked out apples, bananas, and oranges. Then she filled her cart with salad fixings; romaine lettuce, tomatoes, a cucumber, and some radishes. She performed this exercise from rote memory because she was still thinking about Lisa and how painful it was when she left. In hindsight, Annie should've known, all the signs were there but Annie was blind. She came to the conclusion that Lisa as never going to stay, this was indicative of when they went shopping and Lisa was never eager to buy anything for the house. Annie later determined that that would've meant joint property and Lisa turned out to be footloose and fancy free. Property would've bogged her down so when it came time to leave, Lisa's entire wardrobe fit in a duffle bag, except for her hang up clothes, those she draped across her back, holding onto the hangers with her hand over her shoulder. Lisa walked out of the bedroom with all of her belongings, stopping long enough to toss the house key on the dining table, and left the condo. Annie never saw her again.

Annie finished her grocery shopping, checked out, and left the store with her bags of food. She located her Nissan Sentra. It was tucked behind a big truck and for a minute she thought, *Great, just great, someone stole my car; as if today couldn't get any worse*. Glad that no one stole her car, she opened the trunk, stowed her bags, and opened the driver's door. She sat in her car for a moment replaying the conversation with Margaret and then the thoughts that she had afterward. A single tear fell down her cheek. She put the key in the ignition, wiped her eyes, and started the car. Before she put the car in drive she said a silent prayer, "I don't know who you are, where you are, or when I'm going to meet you, but I can't find you soon enough." Annie quietly drove back to her condo.

She pulled into her reserved parking spot that came free with the condo, she could have paid for an extra space if she wanted one, but there was no need. The minimal visitors she had could easily park in the allotted visitor parking spaces for the complex, besides Annie did not want to spend the extra fifty dollars a month for a space that might not even be near her unit. She did remember that she paid for Lisa to have her own parking space and luckily, they were able to secure a space just 3 spaces from Annie's. Now that Annie thought about it, Lisa never paid to park there; Annie had always picked up that tab. Annie sat in her car and became infuriated with herself when she began to mentally tick away all of the things that she had purchased for Lisa, or the cash she had given her because she was running a little short, or the Christmas gifts that she bought for Lisa's family because Lisa thought they would be great coming from Annie. *No sense in crying over spilled milk,* she thought to herself. There was nothing she could do about it anyway; she had already recouped her losses over the last two years and had begun building up a nice little nest egg. She was proud of her financial gains but remained frugal in order to keep saving her money. She also invested in the school's 403B Retirement Plan and at 27 years old she had accumulated thirty thousand in her savings account and almost eighty thousand in her 403B. If she wanted to take a trip, she had the where with all to do it. She thought about taking a short trip to the mountains to go camping or stay in a cabin and the thought brightened her spirits.

The car started getting hot and Annie realized that she had been sitting there just daydreaming about taking a trip, all the while the New Mexico sun beat down on her car. She immediately remembered her dairy products and produce curdling and wilting in the trunk. She exited her vehicle and turned toward the back of the car when a neighbor raised their hand to wave at her. She waved back and unlocked her trunk to fetch her bags when she felt someone near her. She turned just in time to keep from knocking down Mrs. Arthur from 1C. Most of the elderly residents lived on the ground floor, leaving floors two and three for the younger people. The complex was mostly made up of single and married couples with no children. The only time there were children on the property was when grandchildren came to visit their grandparents and because most of the grandparents lived on the ground floor, the kids would be let loose without supervision. This meant that the kids could play hide and seek, hopscotch, jump rope, or basketball. It didn't matter what they were playing, they always seemed to make a lot of noise doing it. It didn't bother Annie. She was used to kids whooping and hollering but some of the other tenants would complain and the manager on duty would have to go talk to an elderly grandparent or two.

Mrs. Arthur stepped back a bit when Annie turned around with her grocery bags as if Annie was going to ask this ninety-year-old woman to help carry her groceries up. Annie was startled to see Mrs. Arthur so close to her when she turned that she took a quick breath. Even more disturbing is how Annie didn't hear Mrs. Arthur approach her, Annie's first thought was, "Geriatric Ninja". Annie shook the thought from her head and politely said, "Good Afternoon Mrs. Arthur, how are you?"

Mrs. Arthur was prim and proper, her hair containing the blue rinse trademark of many elderly ladies, her dress freshly pressed, her sensible walking shoes polished and without a speck of dirt on them, and her modest jewelry sparkling in the sun.

She squinted her eyes as if the sun was blinding her, even though she was facing the shade, and demurely stated, "The condo association is looking for a new president and many of us tenants think that you would be a wonderful candidate for the position. What do you think dear?"

Annie moved into the condo about four years ago and had attended a few of the association meetings so she was aware of the President's responsibility and really didn't want to have any part of it.

As she stood there with her bags of groceries, she extended her biggest smile to Mrs. Arthur and said, "Although I'm very flattered that you thought of me, I think I'm going to have to decline. This school year is terribly busy, and I have twelve more students then I should have, so my time is spent grading homework lessons and attending parent teacher conferences in the evening."

Mrs. Arthur pursed her lips and raised one eyebrow and said, "Well, everyone who lives here has to take a turn at being President. Why don't you take the position and just get in out of the way?"

Annie's groceries, which were getting heavy in her arms, (*mental note: work out upper body more*) again, with all of the syrupy politeness she could muster, said, "I really don't think so Mrs. Arthur. Don't you think that Nick and Angela Morris would be better suited? If we had a married President, the spouse could always cover when the President couldn't make the meetings. I'm single and really don't have the time or energy to be the Condo Association President."

This was all the fodder Mrs. Arthur needed, she quipped, "Oh, that's right, that lovely young lady that lived with you for awhile moved out a couple of years ago didn't she? What was her name? Lilly? Linda? Lucy?" Before Mrs. Arthur listed every "L" name in the Big Book of Baby Names for Expectant Mothers, Annie interjected, "Lisa, her name was Lisa."

Mrs. Arthur began nodding her head vigorously, "Yes, Yes, Lisa, she was a dear one, always helpful, offering to carry groceries, take out the rubbish when she went, holding doors. We could've used a lot more tenants like her around this place that's for sure."

Annie didn't know what to say. This is the second time in one day that Lisa's name had been mentioned and, in both instances, she was portrayed in a positive light. What fresh Hell did Annie step into today when she left her condo to go to the market? She felt like she had fallen in the "Lisa Cunningham Twilight Zone" and all she knew was that she needed to get away from this lady and any more thoughts or discussions of her ex. Annie could feel the paper bags getting wet from the condensation coming off of the refrigerated items and kindly made her leave of Mrs. Arthur.

Annie walked through the courtyard and trudged up the stairs to her condo. For the first time since she moved in, she didn't like it here, there were too many memories. She had lived with her Mom in order to save up the money to put a down payment on it and at 23, she was a fully-fledged property owner and she was proud of this accomplishment. Six months later she met Lisa and after three months of dating, they decided that two could live cheaper than one, so they moved in together. Annie thought she had hit the mother lode. She had a good job, a nice condo, and a girl that loved her; what could go wrong? Fifteen months later all hell broke loose in Annie's world when she decided to empty the dishwasher. *ENOUGH!* Annie screamed in her mind and busied herself with putting her groceries in the fridge.

After the groceries were stowed, Annie desperately needed a shower. She wanted to wash the emotional grime that seemed to cover her body. As she walked through the bedroom to the Master Bath, she noticed that she had thrown her laundry on the bed in preparation to fold it, but that would have to wait. All Annie could think about was having hot water and suds cleanse her body and if she could open her skull, she would wash her brain too in hopes of ridding her mind of the terrible memories that she had experienced that day. The water was hot and steamy when she climbed into the shower and immediately grabbed her loofa and body wash. She routinely put the wash on the loofa and began scrubbing her body like a mad woman; she just couldn't get clean enough. Her skin, usually golden and tan, was bright red when she finished her shower due to a combination of too hot water and a loofa that felt like sandpaper against her skin. Satisfied that the emotional baggage slid down the drain with the rest of the soap and water, she grabbed her towel off of the hook and dried her body. She stepped out of the shower and picked up her body lotion and began massaging it into her skin. This was one of her favorite lotions; it smelled of cocoa butter and reminded her of the beach, even though it had been years since she had been to the beach, when the scent of the lotion hit her olfactory, she was transported back in time when she learned how to surf and boogie board. It was the summer after she graduated from college and it was the best summer of her life, or so she thought, but a new summer was on the horizon.

A summer was on the way that would bring rays of sunshine that shone beyond comprehension, a summer full of heat, passion, joy, and laughter.

Chapter 7

"School Daze"

Annie had the distinct pleasure of working in one of the newer elementary schools in the Albuquerque Public School District. She taught 5th Grade in the Georgia O'Keefe (GOK) Elementary School building located on San Victoria Avenue. The building was built in 1989, making it in the top ten newest elementary schools in the district. Their mascot was the Ram and depending on the procreation habits of parents with cabin fever, the attendance could fluctuate between 595 and 620 students. Founded in 1891, Annie's school district was the largest of 89 public school districts in the state of New Mexico. Within the first decade of 2000 it had a total of 143 schools with some 95,000 students, making it one of the largest school districts in the United States. That number had either doubled or was close to doubling and was indicative of the number of students that she had her class this year. Of the some 20,000 children that make up the school district, 66% are Hispanic, 21% are White, 5% are American Indian, 3% are Black, and 2% are Asian. Ethnicity meant nothing to Annie, she saw all of her kids as one color and that color was "student". Her class this year had 35 students and they were all crammed in her room like little sardines, even though the state average was 15 students per teacher and she normally had a class size of 25. Annie often wondered where the statisticians gleaned their data from because she had not had a class size of 15 since she started working for the district right out of college. She had been with the district for 5 years now and had always taught 5th grade at GOK. She had been there long enough to have taught siblings and was always delighted when one of her new students said, "You taught my brother (or sister) and they said you was nice." Not having the heart to correct the child's grammar, she politely said, "Thank you, and I know you are going to be just as smart if not smarter than they were." This always brought a smile to the child's face as they scampered off, thinking that they were going to "one up" their brother or sister.

Annie parked her Nissan in the faculty parking lot, got out of her vehicle, and walked around to the passenger side to retrieve her book bag and purse. She called it a book bag but it was really a soft sided briefcase for when she went on trips and took her laptop. Now she used it to carry papers back and forth when she took work home with her. Today, her book bag was full of the 35 essays that she spent the weekend grading. She shut the door, clicked the lock button on her remote, and listened as the horn tooted to tell her the Sentra was locked up safely. Buses were beginning to drop off students with the little ones, first and second graders, being dropped off first, the next set of buses would drop off the third and fourth graders, and finally, the last set of buses would drop of the fifth and sixth graders. Annie still had plenty of time to get her coffee and prepare her lesson plans before her students even arrived at the building. She briskly walked to the front door of the school house and quickly entered to escape the morning heat, it was going to be another hot day in New Mexico today and she was glad that her building had central air conditioning. Some of the older buildings in the district still used window units which did nothing more than crank out hot air and the kids were miserable and none of the teachers wore makeup because it usually ended up running down their faces by the end of the day. Yes, Annie considered herself lucky.

Annie made the short walk to the office to check her mail and then stopped by the Teacher's

Lounge to have a cup of coffee before she headed to class. She usually had one to two cups but this morning was only a one cup kind of day. She was running later than usual, she didn't sleep well the night before and had vivid dreams of Commitment Ceremonies and dishwashers. She put her lunch sack in the common fridge and sat down at the large table to enjoy her coffee.

She saddled up next to Maria Gonzales who taught 6th grade and said, "Good morning Maria, did you have a nice weekend?" Maria was a portly woman whose body shook all over when she laughed and she was always laughing and Annie loved this about her. If she was having a bad day she would seek out Maria and within minutes, Annie's sour mood did an immediate about face and she was laughing right along with Maria. Maria had a beautiful Hispanic face that was flawless and wrinkle free even though she was in her fifties. Her black hair matched her eyes and she wore deep red lipstick on her full lips. Annie was always envious of Maria's lips; she wished her own lips were as plump and full as Maria's. Not that she had thin lips because she didn't, she just wanted them fuller.

Maria looked at Annie with a gleam in her eye and said, "I had a wonderful weekend, my cousin Jose came over and brought a few of his friends and we had a cookout, some cerveza, some sangria, it was mucho fun." Annie smiled because Maria had no problems "outing" her cousin Jose as a big ole Queen. It warmed Annie's heart to know that Maria supported her gay cousin because it was typically frowned upon in the strict Catholic Hispanic community. Maria was proud of her cousin and his accomplishments; he went to college and became an IT Manager and she welcomed him and his friends into her home at every opportunity. Maria was the only person at GOK that knew of Annie's sexual preference and that was A OK with Annie; she didn't want her personal business out on the street in the event that one of her students learned of it.

Maria leaned over and with a twinkle in her eye, said, "One of Jose's friends came over with him and SHE is single." Annie just started shaking her head. There were still a couple of teachers lingering in the lounge and Annie hoped that Maria would interpret her head shake as, "Not here, not now."

However, Maria was not to be deterred. She told Annie, "Come on girl, it's been two years, you need to get back out there and mingle."

Annie, ever being polite, replied, "I'm very happy with my life right now".

Maria said, "Not true. I see how sad you are even when you paste that big smile on your face; it doesn't touch your eyes. You're lonely and I can see it." The two teachers that lingered made their exit and this seemed to excite Maria because now she could speak freely and give Annie all the details on the friend that Jose had brought to the cookout.

Maria said, "I met this gal, she is very nice and polite. You two would get along fabulously. Why don't you give it a try?"

Annie shook her head again and said, "I'm just not ready to date. It takes too much energy and right now the only energy I have is for my students."

Maria asked her, "Are you still running three miles a day?"

Annie frowned and said, "Yes, what does that have to do with anything?"

Maria dismissed the question and went on to say, "If you have the energy to run three miles a day, then you have the energy to go out to dinner."

Annie sipped her coffee and began to busy her hands with the placemat that lay in front of her.

Maria reached over and stopped Annie's hand from fiddling and said, "Please, you've got to get back to the world of the living. I'm afraid you're going to end up like old Miss Malewski, an old bitter spinster."

Miss Malewski taught typing to the sixth graders and was the brunt of many Old Maid jokes that circulated the class. She wore her brown hair modestly to her shoulders and it was commonly referred to as the "Football Helmet". Her batwing eyeglasses were still stuck in the 1960's, and most of her clothes consisted of brown polyester pants and a black top. She never joked or laughed with her students and her lips formed a thin flat line across her face.

Annie shuddered and said, "No, I will never end up like Miss Malewski".

Maria raised her eyebrows as if to say, "Wanna bet?" In a last ditch effort, Maria asked, "Well, will you at least think about it?"

Annie grinned and said, "If I say I will think about it, will you drop the subject."

Maria's eyes widened and she retorted, "That's not fair."

Annie chuckled, "Why isn't it fair?"

Maria stated, "Because I have to drop the subject if you say you will think about it, of which I know you won't, and then I am left with a dropped subject! No fair!"

Annie scooted her chair closer to Maria and whispered, "I'll think about it." And with that, Annie finished her coffee, rinsed her cup in the sink and waved goodbye to Maria.

Annie headed to her class room, making her way through a sea of little heads as the first and second graders shuffled to class. She noticed that her student's art work was hanging on the big bulletin board in the hallway and this made her proud. She really liked Kate Roark, the school's Art Teacher, and admired her ability to get the kids to want to do art. Even though she was small in stature, Kate Roark was a force to be reckoned with and actually believed that art was just as important as the most complex mathematical problem or the ability to diagram a sentence. She commanded respect just by entering the room but not in an authoritarian way. All the kids loved her and wanted to do good by her which was plain to see from the collages, the drawings, and paintings that adorned the bulletin board. Annie thought that Kate's height had a lot to do with earning the respect of the students. Standing a mere five foot tall, Kate was the same height as many of the students and they perceived her as less threatening than the taller teachers. Annie took one last look at the art and opened the door to her class.

The room was dimly lit with just the sun peeking through the windows. This was her favorite time to be in her room. She still couldn't believe that this was her classroom. In fact, she still had to pinch herself every once in awhile to bring herself back to reality and that this just wasn't a dream that she had 5 years ago. Without having to look, she reached out and turned on the overhead lights and set her book bag briefcase on her desk. She walked over and said good morning to Milton, the class ferret, and noticed that he was in need of food. She would make sure that one of the kids fed him first thing when they got here. It was their responsibility to take care of Milton and so far, they had taken this responsibility seriously. Milton still had his hair and that was a bonus considering last year's ferret didn't fare as well.

She returned to her desk, unzipped her book bag briefcase, and extracted the papers that she had graded over the weekend. She sat them in a neat pile on her desk ready to be handed out when class began. She had prepared her lesson plan the previous Friday but two days had passed so she quickly perused the content and was pleased with what she had prepared. She had a good group of kids this year and they were surpassing the academic progress criteria for the state. Most of her students fell into the 38% Above Average for both the District and the State. This was an accomplishment that she took credit for; she gave all accolades to her students for putting in the time and effort into their homework and extra credit. There were a couple of students that needed one on one time with her but the majority of the kids just "got it" and all Annie had to do was lecture, start conversations, and arbitrate when discussions got a little heated. She presented the material and the kids took to it like a fish in water. She looked at the clock and at that same exact moment the bell rang and her kids started pouring into the classroom, making their way to their desks. They said, "Good Morning Miss Monroe." She responded in kind. She noticed that Isabella was wearing the same clothes that she wore on Friday and gave a stern "Shush" when the other girls giggled at her. Juan swiftly moved between Isabella and the other girls and muttered to Isabella, "They're jerks". Isabella gave Juan a small smile and sat down at her desk. Annie remembered that it was Juan's paper that she upgraded to a "B" due to his volatile home life which is why he probably felt the need to protect Isabella.

Five minutes after the bell rang, all students were in their assigned seats and Annie began taking roll call. Seventy five percent of her class was Hispanic and the other twenty five percent was a melting pot of Caucasian and Black. Annie didn't know Spanish and when the students wanted to pull the wool over her eyes, they automatically began speaking in their native language.

Maria was the school Spanish teacher and Annie still couldn't figure that one out, "Why do we have a Spanish Teacher when all of the kids already speak Spanish." Maria said that her purpose was to teach the other 25 percent which included Annie. Before she began class, she asked Jorge to feed Milton.

Jorge rose from his desk, looked at Annie, and asked, "Miss Monroe, why does Milton have a white name?" Confronted with an issue that could quickly escalate to racism she merely looked at Jorge and said, "That was his name when we got him so that is his name. Why do you have a Hispanic name?"

Jorge grinned and said, "Maybe because I'm Spanish." There were chuckles throughout the room and all Annie could do was say, "Good One. Now feed Milton so we can begin class."

Jorge did as instructed and returned to his desk.

Annie picked up the papers and began handing out the essays. She could see the fear in Juan's eyes when she approached his desk and it looked as though they were welling with tears. She handed him the paper and said, "Good job Juan". Juan blinked his tears away and kindly said, "Thank you Miss Monroe." He knew that he hadn't given the paper his best effort but once again, Miss Monroe saved him from a fate worse than death had he brought home a "C".

She next handed Jose Garcia his paper and he really did get a "C", so she gave him some words of encouragement about next time, "I know you can do it Jose."

Jose raised a hand and stated rather matter of factly, "It's Joe."

Annie raised her eyebrows and inquired as to why Jose wanted to be called Joe. His answer tore a hole right through her heart, he said, "Well, white people get all of the good jobs so if I start going by Joe now, maybe by the time I start working people will know me as Joe instead of the seeing the color of my skin."

Annie didn't have an answer for Jose/Joe. She finished handing out the papers then instructed the class to get out their English books to begin today's lesson.

The rest of the morning went by without any turbulence and Annie was glad to see that it was almost lunch time. She and Maria shared cafeteria duty but today was their day off so they found each other in the Teacher's Lounge. Annie grabbed her sack from the fridge and Maria took out a container that had some type of meat in it and began warming it up in the microwave. Annie sat in her usual spot as Maria tended to her lunch, which really made Annie's stomach rumble. Whatever she had brought smelled delicious and very spicy. Annie opened her yogurt and Maria turned to face her.

Maria stood there with her hands on her hips and asked, "Well?"

"Well what?" Annie asked, swallowing a bite of yogurt.

"You know well what! Did you think about the date?" Maria whispered, her eyes narrowing.

Annie thought to herself, *My God, this woman is relentless*.

She had to confess to Maria that she had not thought about it but would ponder the possibility tonight at home and promised to have an answer for her tomorrow. Maria accepted this and not another word was said about "The Date".

The rest of the day passed with successes and failures but overall, it was a good afternoon and Annie was pleased with her kids' efforts. The final bell rang and the kids scrambled for the door, leaving Annie yelling, "Hey, don't forget to start your book reports!"

She peeked in on Milton and made sure he had plenty of food and water for overnight, and then she grabbed her book bag briefcase and started out of the building to her car. She was about half way home when she remembered to think about "The Date". She thought to herself that she hadn't had a smile in a little while and that maybe just one dinner date wouldn't hurt. The mere thought of ending up like old Miss Malewski gave her shudders and she just couldn't have that at twenty seven years old. She let herself daydream about someone opening her car door for her, bringing her flowers (maybe), and paying for dinner. She had had enough of going Dutch and splitting the dinner check. She was of a mindset that if whoever does the asking for the date is also the one that should be picking up the bill. As she eased her Nissan into her parking space she had decided that she would make Maria happy and go on a blind date. Once the decision was made, Annie stepped a little lighter and her spirits lifted a bit. She was actually going to look forward to going out. Maybe her social luck was taking a turn for the better. She sure hoped so.

Chapter 8

"Annie's Blind Date"

Annie jerked awake with a start. She was covered with sweat, tangled in the bed sheets, her heart racing. She ran her shaking fingers through her hair and tried desperately to forget the bad dream she just woke from. In her dream she was running through a grocery store trying to evade Lisa who was chasing her. In the dream, Lisa kept saying, "Stop, I need to talk to you." Annie kept running and Lisa kept chasing her. Lisa yelled, "Come on Annie, stop, it's not bad news." In her dream, Annie could see a figure standing at the end of the aisle, she was hoping that whoever the person was, would help her. The outline showed a very large person and Annie was sure that this man could stop Lisa before she caught her. As she drew closer to the end of the aisle, she realized that this wasn't a man at all, it was Margaret.

Margaret stood there menacingly as Annie approached her. Annie tried to stop short of running into Margaret, but it was too late, Margaret caught her in a firm embrace. Margaret turned Annie around to face Lisa and yelled, "Here she is Lisa. I got her for ya!" Annie looked in horror as Lisa reached out to grab Annie from Margaret and at that same exact moment, Annie woke up from the nightmare.

She sat for a minute in her bed, recognizing her surroundings she thought, "*Damn that woman, I'm tired of her renting space in my head.*" The dream woke her up before her alarm went off, so she reached over and slid the button to "off", untangled her legs from the sheets and got out of bed. She headed straight for the bathroom to relieve herself and caught a glimpse of her image in the mirror. Her hair was plastered to her scalp from sweating, her face was ashen, and her eyes were dull. She would have to spend a little bit of extra time getting ready for work if she had any hopes of improving her looks before school. She pulled down her shorts and sat on the toilet. It took a minute for her stream to start as she rehashed the dream she just woke from. It was a disturbing dream and even though she was not one for dream interpretation, she wondered if the conversation at the market with Margaret and now this dream meant that she would be running into Lisa anytime in the near future. These thoughts lead her to remember that she had her blind date tonight. Ugh!

She wiped, stood up, flushed the toilet, and tossed her shorts aside as she turned on the shower. She couldn't wait to get clean and wash the dream down the drain. She took off her tee shirt, threw it on top of the shorts, and stepped into the shower. She quickly bathed herself, grabbed her towel off of the hook, and stepped out of the shower. She didn't have time to dilly dally this morning; she needed to work on the bags under her eyes. She wrapped the towel around her, brushed her teeth, and headed to the kitchen. She needed coffee big time. She popped the K-cup in her Kuerig and hit the start button. Her cup had been neatly placed on the tray the night before. Within seconds, the machine started to spurt coffee into her mug. It gurgled and hissed as it finished its cycle and within a minute, she was sipping a comforting cup of java. She turned away from the kitchen counter and shuffled to her bedroom to get dressed for her day in front of twenty-seven eager faces that were ready to test her limits.

Annie placed her coffee cup on the nightstand and turned to enter her walk-in closet. If the truth be known, this was the reason that she even bought this condo. It had a large walk in closet with shelves, drawers, hanging bars, and cubbies for her shoes. Yes, this was the best room in the entire condo.

The weather was going to be warm that day, so she went straight to her dresses and began flipping hangers. She settled on a Lilly Pulitzer shift and a pair of open toed nude flat sandals. She liked her sleeveless shift dresses and she had the right body for their cut and length. Her arms were shapely and tanned as was the rest of her body. Her legs extended below the hem that touched her thigh right above her knee cap. Yes, this was the best outfit for the day. Now, to work on the face; she picked up her mug and made her way back to the bathroom. She pulled out her hairdryer, bent at the waist, flipped her hair forward, and began drying her honey golden hair. When her hand no longer felt dampness, she turned her dryer off and flipped her hair back as she stood up. Her beautiful blonde tresses falling around her shoulders as her hair formed a halo around her face. Full of volume from the hairdryer, her hair looked like a lion's mane. She picked up her brush and tamed the wild curls. Once her hair was manageable, she turned her focus to her face. She applied her moisturizer and could see that the bags that were previously hanging below her eyes, had dissipated and were gone. She dabbed on her foundation and lightly brushed on rouge to brighten her cheeks. She chose a smoky eye shadow and brushed mascara on her eyelashes. She finished with a light pink lip stick and was happy with the outcome as she blotted her lips. She could now face her students without trepidation. She wondered if this outfit would be ok for the date, she dreaded having to belabor another outfit. In fact, she was belaboring the date.

Annie turned off the vanity lights above the sink, picked up her coffee cup, and returned to the kitchen. She rinsed out her cup and placed it in the dish strainer, grabbed her purse and book bag briefcase, took her keys off of the hook by the door and stepped out into the bright New Mexico sun. She descended the stairs and made the short walk to her Nissan. She opened the passenger side door and stowed her purse and book bag. She walked around the car and climbed into the driver seat; it was already hotter than hell and she was beginning to perspire so she quickly blasted the AC.

Annie parked in her usual spot at school, took her purse and book bag from the passenger seat, and walked into the building. Finally Friday and she had no papers to grade this weekend. As she made her way to the office to check her mail, Maria came bounding down the hallway with an excited look on her face.

In an eager voice Maria asked, "Well? Are you ready?"

Annie frowned and asked, "Ready for what?"

Maria shook her head and said, "Don't be coy, for your date this evening? Aren't you anxious to meet Kelly? Do you know what you're doing? Or where you're going? What time is she picking you up?"

The questions came out of Maria's mouth in rapid fire succession. Annie didn't remember Maria even taking a breath between questions. Annie rolled her eyes and pushed open the door to the office. She said good morning to Aunt Bea, the school secretary. Beatrice had been the school secretary for over 25 years and had been there long enough to see students grow up and become parents and then enroll their children in the same school. Everyone called her Aunt Bea because she had an uncanny resemblance to Aunt Bea on "The Andy Griffith Show". This was a black and white sitcom that aired in the 1960's and Aunt Bea was probably old enough to remember it. Beatrice returned the pleasantry and turned back to her desk. Annie checked her mail, all the while Maria was fluttering around her like a baby bird learning how to fly.

Maria excitedly asked, "Come on, Come on, what are you going to wear? Don't wear that dress, it's not sexy enough. Are you going to wear heels or flats? Do gay women like women in heels? I think you should wear flats, Kelly is shorter than you. Where that nice dress you wore to the District Banquet last year, you received many compliments on that dress. Or do you think that dress is too dressy?" The woman was relentless thought Annie.

She turned to face Maria and said, "Maria, I love you like a sister, but I just really need you to shut up right now." Maria abruptly stopped talking and mumbled an apology. It wasn't like Annie to be so stern with anyone, so her statement took Maria off guard.

In a softer and calmer voice, Maria said, "I'm just so excited for you and want to see you back in the dating scene rather than throwing yourself into your work all of the time."

Annie relaxed and in a more gentle voice said, "I'm sorry, I know that you are just happy for me but really, it's no big deal. Plus, I didn't sleep well and woke up from a bad dream about Lisa." Maria didn't take this news too well; she had little or no regard for Lisa Cunningham and what she did to Annie. It was Maria who listened to Annie sob. It was Maria who held Annie when her world was falling apart. It was Maria who had been there and helped Annie work through the stages of grief. If she never heard the name Lisa Cunningham, it would be too soon.

Annie left the office, saying good day to Aunt Bea, and turned toward her classroom instead of going to the Teacher's Lounge to have her second cup of coffee. She knew that Maria would probably follow her and at this time of the morning, Annie just couldn't take much more of Maria and her Spanish Inquisition. She opened the door to her classroom and immediately felt peace. She walked over and said good morning to Milton and filled his water dish. She went back to her desk and pulled out her lesson plans for the day. It was going to be an easy day for both her and her students. They had been working hard at preparing for their state scholastic exams and she was proud of them. They deserved a light day and so did she. She didn't know if she could handle a heavy class day on top of the date that was looming in the near future.

With Annie's permission, Maria gave Kelly her phone number so the two of them could connect and get to know each other over the phone before meeting in person. Kelly called her the same day that Maria had given her Annie's number. They exchanged pleasantries and talked long enough to learn about family and friends; their likes and dislikes and whether or not a date could be arranged. Annie agreed to have dinner with Kelly before she hung up the phone. Kelly wanted to pick her up, but Annie thought it would be best if they met at a predetermined location, so they agreed to meet at the new Sushi Bar near the mall at 7:00 Friday evening.

The morning hours passed quickly with the kids happy that their lessons were not as taxing as they had been the previous four days. Milton got taken out of his cage and passed around like a new puppy, spending time with each student that wanted to hold him. Some of the girls were convinced that Milton was a rat and wanted nothing to do with him. There was one boy, Earl, who absolutely adored Milton and when he got to hold him, he was hard pressed to let go of him. Earl didn't like to share Milton and he was always the first one to say hello to the little furry ferret in the morning and the last to say goodbye at the end of the day before he went home. Earl loved Milton. At exactly 11:45 the bell rang signaling lunch for the 5th graders. The 5th and 6th grade classes were allowed to go the cafeteria on their own without having to go as a group like the younger classes. Annie had cafeteria duty that day with Maria and was in hopes that Maria had curbed her enthusiasm over Annie's social life. Annie left her classroom and followed her students down the hall to the cafeteria.

Annie didn't bring her lunch on days that she was a Cafeteria Proctor; she would eat whatever hot lunch was being served to the kids. The Proctors had a table in the back corner of the cafeteria where they could oversee the students eating their lunches in order to make sure there was nothing awry during the lunch period. The Proctors would ensure there were no food fights and that none of the younger children had their lunch taken from them by an older student. Annie noticed that most of the kids were subdued and the cafeteria wasn't as boisterous as usual. This was probably due to all grades preparing for the state exams and all of the kids were just exhausted. Annie got in line behind two of her students, picked up a tray and silverware, and waited to be served. She held her sectioned tray under the glass and it was filled with the entrée, vegetables, and dessert. Today's culinary delight was chicken ala king, steamed carrots, and for dessert, apple crisp. The food actually smelled good to Annie, she was hungry, and had left her condo without as much as a piece of fruit for the ride into work. She took her tray to the Proctor table and sat down. She unfolded her napkin and placed it in her lap, took a sip of iced tea, and looked up just in time to see Maria waddling down the aisle between two sets of tables, her own tray in hand. Annie and Maria had proctored the lunchroom for the entire five years that Annie had been at the school and for the most part, she enjoyed Maria's company. However, today may not be one of those days. Maria set her tray down across from Annie and put her hand up. She said, "I promise not to say a word about your date tonight." Annie looked at her and said, "You just did."

They finished their lunches in relative silence, Maria chomping at the bit to talk about Kelly but wouldn't go back on her word. Annie just kept scanning the lunchroom, making sure that the kids were behaving themselves. Annie could feel the nagging signs of a headache coming on and for a split second thought about calling Kelly and cancelling their date, but Kelly had sounded so upbeat and excited about their date that Annie didn't have the heart to call her and beg off with the oldest affliction known to man or woman... a headache. Lunch ended without too much hoopla, Maria took both Annie's and her trays up to the conveyor that would take the dirty dishes into the kitchen to be washed. They both turned to leave the cafeteria and Maria took Annie's arm in her hand and said, "Please try to have a good time, Kelly is a nice gal." Annie nodded compliance and with that, Maria turned and walked down the hallway to her own classroom. Annie turned and walked in the opposite direction.

The afternoon went even quicker than the morning and Annie began to feel the first flickers of anxiety about her blind date. During class, Annie broke up the students into groups and passed out crossword puzzles of science and nature, English literature, and History. She allowed the kids to work on the puzzles as a group and talking amongst them was allowed. She encouraged them to work as a team to solve the puzzles. The first team to solve their puzzles correctly was allowed to finish their class time in the library and they would be dismissed from there. Twenty-seven little heads bent over the puzzles to solve them so that they could go to the library. The afternoon passes with hushed tones coming from desk tops as the kids worked their puzzles. Earl's group was the first group to finish. Annie graded their work and nodded that they were free to go and that she would see them bright and early on Monday. The team quickly rose from their desks, grabbed their backpacks and was headed for the door except for Earl, who approached Annie's desk. He had a favor to ask and inquired, "Miss Monroe, can I stay here and sit with Milton instead of going to the library." Annie admired his request but thought it was best if he joined his team in the library. He put his head down and said, "Ok, have a nice weekend Miss Monroe."

The other two groups were still working on their puzzles when the final bell rang for dismissal. Desks were quickly scooted back into their appointed positions, book bags were pulled out, and the students pushed toward the door. Goodbyes were being said and several kids yelled at Miss Monroe to have a good weekend. Annie waved to no one in particular and wished them a good weekend as well. She walked up and down each row of desks like a flight attendant on an airplane, making sure that no one left any personal belongings. She checked in on Milton, making sure he had plenty of food and water for the weekend. One of the kids usually took Milton home to their house over the weekend but there were no takers today so Milton would spend the weekend in his cage and the janitor would check on him again before he went home. Annie approached her desk, put the class history and math books in her book bag, took her purse from her bottom desk drawer and slowly walked to the door. She hesitated before she turned the lights off and took one last look around, all was well, and she flipped the switch.

Annie's ride home was stop and go due to traffic. She usually found herself wedged between two school busses for the better part of her drive home, so she made a last minute decision to pick up her dry cleaning. The dry cleaner was in a strip mall where she got her hair trimmed and nails manicured. She thought about stopping in the salon to get her ends trimmed but thought better of it. It was already four o'clock and she wanted to give herself ample time to stress over her date. She would have to leave the condo at six to make it to the mall in time. She gave the clerk her stub and he came back with her sweaters and a jacket that she had dropped off the previous week. She paid the man, thanked him, and turned to leave the store. After putting her dry cleaning in the car, she thought again about her hair and decided that maybe a trim wouldn't hurt. She shut the car door, walked next door to the salon, and asked Amy if she had time for a walk in. Amy nodded and asked, "Ten minutes?" Annie nodded back in return and took a seat in the waiting area. She reached over and picked up the latest gossip magazine and learned that a certain prince was marrying a Hollywood actress and that it would be the wedding of the century. She thought, "That's great, at least someone is getting married, because it sure wasn't her." The article turned her thoughts to her date and for a minute she was hopeful. Maria had nothing but positive things to say about Kelly and Annie was secretly hoping that they hit it off. Even though she was wary of jumping into anything, she was tired of being lonely.

It was almost five o'clock when she climbed back into her car and had a moment of panic about not having enough time to get ready. She wasted no time driving home. She parked her car, grabbed her belongings, and skipped up the stairs to her condo. Balancing her purse, book bag, and dry cleaning she unlocked her door and entered the cool foyer. She hooked her keys, dropped her purse on the kitchen counter, and went to her closet. Annie removed the plastic from her dry cleaning and put the clothes away. She turned, went into the bathroom and turned on the shower. As the water began to heat up, she deftly reached around and unzipped her dress, her mind began to think of how nice it would be to have someone unzip her dress for her and she created an image of Kelly in her mind.

She envisioned Kelly to be shorter than her but only slightly. Annie stood 5'7" and most of her height was due to her long legs. In Annie's fantasy, Kelly was lean and trim; she had an athletic body of which Annie was attracted. Kelly would have shoulder length hair and sparkling blue eyes. Kelly was cute in a sporty kind of way; not butch but rather more on the femme side. Annie was not attracted to manly looking women. It's not that she had anything against women who chose to look a certain way, she just knew what she wanted and she wanted someone who looked more womanly, she was after all, a lesbian who enjoyed women.

She quickly removed her makeup and stepped into the shower for a quick cleanse. She washed and rinsed her hair and took her towel off of the hook. After drying off, she wrapped the towel around her, put her hair up in another towel and padded into her closet. "Now what do I wear" she silently asked herself. She went over to where her slacks hung and decided on a nice pair of black slacks that would accentuate her height. She crossed the room and chose a white silk button down shirt and a black bolero sweater. The evenings could get chilly in the desert and she didn't want to get cold. She selected a nice pair of black shoes with a kitten heel; she didn't want to appear too tall. Happy with her selection, Annie returned to the bathroom to dry her hair and re-apply her makeup. She chose a classic loop earring, a matching necklace, and thin bangles to place on her wrist. She dressed quickly and looked at the clock; she was relieved that she would actually be early for her date which pleased her because she never wanted to be late for anything. The last touch was a dab of Hermes cologne behind her ears and she was ready. She transferred her wallet, lipstick, and breath mints from her purse to a silver clutch and left her condo. She was glad that she chose to wear a short sweater because the sun was beginning to set and the desert air would prove to be cool. She got in her car and drove to the sushi bar.

Annie parked her car in the closest spot near the restaurant and proceeded to enter. As soon as she walked in, heads turned. She was a striking figure of a woman even if just wearing black slacks and a white blouse. It was not about what she was wearing but more about how she carried herself. Annie had a regal quality about her. She walked straight, head held high, and more or less glided rather than walked. One could not help but notice her when she entered a room.

She approached the hostess, smiled, and said, "A table for two".

The hostess lead Annie to a table in the middle of the restaurant and Annie quickly asked, "Do you have a booth available?"

The hostess turned and said, "Of course, right this way."

Annie took the side that faced the door so she would be able to look at the patrons who entered, secretly wondering if she would be able to pick out Kelly when she walked through the door.

A waitress brought a glass of water to the table and Annie quickly said, "We will need two glasses." Annie smiled to herself at the thought of two glasses of water and the idea of not being alone.

Annie unrolled her napkin, removed the silverware and chopsticks, and placed the napkin in her lap as she patiently waited for Kelly. Several couples came through the door and Annie paid no attention to the men but rather took in what each of the women were wearing, especially the shoes. One could tell a lot about a woman by the shoes that she wore.

Annie sipped her water when she noticed a short, stocky woman enter the restaurant and panicked. *"Oh please don't let this be Kelly!"*

The woman had short cropped hair that was heavily gelled and sticking straight up in short spikes. She wore khaki pants, a white polo shirt with short sleeves, and a plaid sweater vest. The pleats at the top of her pants slightly bulged with the weight of her stomach, and she wore a pair of scuffed loafers on her pudgy feet. There was no place to run and Annie sat frozen in the booth. If this was Kelly, she was the epitome of every woman that Annie was not attracted to. Ever being the class act, Annie pasted on her best smile as Kelly approached grinning from ear to ear. Kelly looked at Annie like a star struck teenager. Annie stood up as Kelly neared the table more out of courtesy than anything else. Kelly misinterpreted this consideration as an opening for an embrace. Annie was taken a little aback but returned the hug none the less. They both sat down in their respective sides of the booth.

Kelly immediately leaned over the table and in a raised voice said, "My God, you are gorgeous. Maria didn't do you justice in the looks department if I say so myself!" Annie smiled and thanked Kelly for the compliment.

Kelly looked as if she wanted Annie to say something similar in return but all Annie could say was, "Do you like sushi?"

Kelly said, "Not really, I don't believe that bait should be for human consumption." After two sentences Annie determined that Kelly expressed herself with a southern drawl which seemed out of place in New Mexico. In light of the accent, Annie found herself asking Kelly if she was from New Mexico.

Kelly replied, "Oh shucks no, I'm from Gulfport, Mississippi." Annie was horrified and immediately began planning her attack on Maria for this entire mess. Annie continued to smile in spite of herself and listened as Kelly rambled on about her job at the automotive plant and that if she played her cards right, she could be promoted to Shift Leader.

Kelly continued to explain her work and added, "If I get this promotion I will get a buck fifty an hour pay raise which will be nice because I need the money now more than ever."

Annie asked if Kelly was in some type of financial bind and Kelly replied, "Oh Gosh no, I will just need the extra money because I plan on asking you out again." Annie hoped that Kelly didn't see her shudder and quickly took a drink of ice water.

The waitress came and asked if they would like cocktails and Kelly piped up first saying, "Yes, the little lady will have a glass of white wine and I'll have a shot of bourbon and a Budweiser." Annie wanted to retract the order for two reasons, 1.) She didn't like white wine or any other wine with sushi, and 2.) She was driving. She let the order stand, not wanting to hurt Kelly's feelings.

She thought to herself, "*This is just going from bad to worse. What's up with a shot of bourbon and a beer?*"

Kelly turned her attention back to Annie and said, "I hope you don't mind me ordering for you, but I'm a take charge kind of gal and whenever I am in the presence of a lady, I want to be as gentlemanly as possible."

Annie's mind screamed, "*OH MY GOD, what have I gotten myself into; Maria, you're a dead woman!*" Ever the lady, Annie just shook her head and said, "No, white wine is fine, thank you." The waitress turned to put their order in at the bar.

Kelly stayed hunched over the table toward Annie and Annie could feel the springs from the booth pressing against her bag as she tried to retreat from Kelly being almost in her face. Kelly decided to make small talk by asking questions about Annie being a teacher and with every question she asked Annie, she had her own comments to add to the conversation.

When Kelly asked Annie if she liked being a teacher, she added, "I didn't go to college. I've always worked blue collar jobs because they are more my speed."

Annie wondered what Kelly's speed actually was and even more important, how was she ever going to make it through dinner with this woman? The waitress brought their drinks and before Annie could even comprehend what was going on, Kelly knocked back the shot and took a swig of beer. Annie was mortified and couldn't believe it when Kelly wiped her mouth with the back of her hand.

The waitress kindly asked Kelly if she would like a glass for her beer and not recognizing the hint at etiquette, Kelly said, "No Ma'am, I'm just fine with the bottle."

Annie thought, "*Maybe I should rethink drinking the wine, I may need it after this.*" The waitress left the menus on the table. Kelly quickly reached for both and handed one to Annie and said, "Allow me." Annie couldn't take much more of the southern gentleman charm and really couldn't believe that she actually stressed over this date. She silently scanned the menu, not wanting to order anything but to just get up and bolt from the restaurant. The waitress returned and once again, Kelly took the lead and ordered Annie the California Roll and herself the Tempura Platter of shrimp and vegetables.

Kelly looked at Annie and said, "Well, at least it's cooked, right?" Annie had no response, in fact, she was speechless. She took a sip of her wine but wanted to guzzle it just to feel the effect. Kelly watched Annie as she took a drink from her wine glass and seemed mesmerized by Annie's lips touching the glass. Annie almost threw up in her mouth when Kelly went, "Mm Mm Mm, my God, you sure are pretty and I wish I was the wine glass." That was the last straw; Annie reached in her clutch and took out her wallet. She laid a twenty and a ten on the table, figuring that would be enough to cover her half of the bill and said to Kelly, "I'm sorry, but I'm not feeling well and need to go." She quickly rose from the booth and made her way to the door, all the while Kelly is saying, "Hey, can I see you again?"

Annie couldn't get into her car fast enough; she quickly turned the ignition, backed out, and sped toward the exit of the parking lot. It wasn't until she was halfway home did she take her foot off of the accelerator. It wasn't like her to just get up and leave from anywhere and she considered herself quite tolerant of most personalities, but she just couldn't take one more word coming out of that woman's mouth. She turned on the radio to drown out the judgmental thoughts that she was having about Kelly. She didn't like to be judgmental and she surely didn't like to stereotype people, but there was a limit to her easy-going nature and perception of people. She did have it within her to label people, no matter how much she tried to fight it. All her mind kept saying was, "That didn't just happen to me and what was Maria thinking?"

Annie drove the rest of the way home with the radio blaring. She pulled into her parking space, sat there for a minute and said out loud to no one, *"Well, so much for getting back into the dating scene."*

Chapter 9

"Views and Messages"

Lynn stretched her arms over her head and her legs straight out as she began to wake up. There was no alarm this morning as it was Saturday and she was glad for the weekend. The week ended on a bad note with the return and she needed some time to decompress and get centered again. She pulled back the black out curtain and saw the sun shining and felt relief; she would be able to get in a bike ride this morning. She continued stretching then threw back the covers and stood up. She went to the bathroom, relieved herself and made her way to the kitchen to start her coffee pot. Everything had been set up the night before so all she had to do was press the button. While the coffee was brewing, she went back to her bedroom and put on her biking shorts and shirt. She didn't bother taking a shower; she would be sweating soon enough. She grabbed a water bottle out of the fridge and her biking shoes that clipped into the pedals for better revolutions per minute. They helped pull the pedal up as much as pushing the pedal down. She didn't bother with coffee, the pot would still be on when she returned from her ride and she would have a cup then. Lynn just wanted to get on her bike and ride again. She grabbed her helmet and extra house key as she left her cabin in the woods.

Lynn secured her helmet and put her feet in the traps on the pedals and coasted down the driveway. She had to maneuver the ruts and pot holes, reminding herself again to call the landscaper to come and grade the drive. She pedaled the short distance down the dirt road, looking at the overgrowth on her property and said out loud, "Someone really ought to do something about that eyesore." She slowed down at the point where the dirt road met the pavement; she looked both ways and then pedaled out into the two-lane country road that abutted her property. Her lot was two and a half acres and mostly woods, in fact, she had no grass to speak of, just trees and many years' worth of fallen leaves. She had lived in the cabin for almost 9 years and couldn't think of living anywhere else. She loved her little town with its one stop light and two stop signs. The Town Hall sat on top of the hill right across from the big Christian Church that rang its bells on Sunday morning. Lynn turned toward the pond and loved this part of her ride. The pond sat between two hills and as long as there were no cars on the road, Lynn could make it down one hill and up the next without having to pedal. Today, she made the hills without incident.

She pedaled toward town, passed the cemetery, the water reservoir, and the stables where she thought about taking riding lessons. Her mind was clear and all she could hear was her own breathing. She neared the intersection of the Town Hall and the Church and shot down Main Street toward the Rail Trail. She came to the second stop sign at the Rail Trail and entered the paved path, she would ride the Trail for about ten miles then turn around and head back home. Once on the Trail she could let her mind wander because she didn't have to pay too close attention to her surroundings. Her thoughts immediately went to Gram, the lady with the pretty smile on the dating website. Lynn spent the next five miles thinking about a picture that she had seen on a dating website. She daydreamed about the two of them having coffee and talking, getting to know one another. She came out of her fugue state around mile six and decided not to do the full ten; she turned around and headed back from whence she came. She had no more thoughts of Gram; she just let the wind blow across her face and thought how wonderful it was to be out on such a gorgeous day. She completed the Rail Trail in record time, maybe it was a good thing to think of the picture of Gram. She turned back up Main Street and went over the bridge where the gravity dam held the Nashua River. She passed the Cumberland Farms and the closed down Chinese Food Restaurant. There were two Chinese Restaurants in the little town and this one was her favorite because they delivered. She rode past the little Food Market and her favorite Sub Shop, the Police Station and the Hardware Store. She slowed down at the rotary but kept in line with the traffic. She pedaled past the Funeral Home and the Library. The Library was the largest building in her town; it was even bigger than the Town Hall. She liked the Library; they were always holding events like "Open Mic Night" and LGBTQ Support Groups for Teens. This pleased Lynn to know that she lived in such a diversified town. She topped the hill in front of the Town Hall and the Church and made the dog leg turn onto the street she lived on. Three more miles and she would've ridden 23 miles that day. Today was a good run. She walked her bike up the driveway when she got home.

Lynn sat on her deck and took off her helmet and bike shoes. She liked her deck. It was large and had room for a Gazebo, table and chairs, and a chaise lounge that she never had lain in. Mental note; work on your tan naturally this summer. She went in the house just as her coffee pot was beeping, signaling that it was about to shut itself off. She punched the "on" button again for another two hours of heated coffee and headed to the bathroom for a shower. She took a cool shower to cool her body down, dried off, and went to her bedroom to don the uniform of the day. Today, she was thinking just a tee shirt and a pair of gym shorts. She put booties on her feet, slipped her feet into her slippers, and went into the kitchen to have her first cup of coffee for the day. She walked passed her desk on her way to the living room, hit the power button to bring her pc to life, and proceeded to catch the morning news on her TV. The top story of the day was how a man under the influence missed a turn and plowed into someone's house. She could figure how that could happen, there were many houses that were very near the roads here in New England. Its' like they literally built the road around the house and a corner of the house would only be about three feet from the road. Some people even put big boulders on the outside of their property to prevent this very thing from happening. She went back to the kitchen to get a yogurt and a granola bar to munch on while she finished watching the news. There was a water main break two towns over from her that was causing a stir, and the Registry of Motor Vehicles would be closed this coming Tuesday so they could do some much needed computer upgrades. She liked her local news, there were hardly ever any stories about violence, or robberies, or murder. It had been ten years since the last murder and that was an elderly man who killed his wife because he no longer recognized her. He had Alzheimer's so there was a legitimate medical problem that caused the killing. Other than that, the news was uneventful. She was more concerned with the weather so she could plan her weekly rides. She was happy to see that rain had been taken out of the forecast.

Lynn pressed the power button on the remote and snapped off the TV. She took her empty yogurt container to the kitchen and tossed it into the trash before she went into her bedroom to empty her hamper and wash a load of clothes. After getting the load in the washing machine, she refilled her coffee cup, and sat down at her computer to check her mail. There were more ads that wanted to sell her vinyl siding, delete. There was an email from the subdivision common drive association telling the whole group of who hadn't paid their dues, how embarrassing, delete. Lynn always paid her dues and wondered why the road was full of potholes. There were four emails from In No Time. She opened the first one and it said that someone once again viewed and liked her profile, delete. Two emails had given her thumbs up, delete.

The last email said she had a message from Gram. It read,

"Hi Lynn, you came in my email as one of the 8 'matches'...... I noticed you live in Pepperell. Nice area; I grew up in Harvard. You have a nice profile. Just thought I'd reach out and let you know. Gram".

Lynn's stomach did a flip and she raised her eyebrows.

She thought to herself, *"Oh my, she contacted me!"*

Lynn responded with, "Good morning! Thank you for liking my email. Maybe we can chat soon. Have a wonderful day! Lynn". Then she immediately identified her mistake and sent another email that said, "I should've said, "Thank you for liking my profile." I'm new here, many apologies. Lynn".

Satisfied that she corrected her error, she went to switch her clothes from the washer to the dryer.

Lynn started her house cleaning chores; she dusted the furniture, vacuumed the area rugs, and mopped the hardwood floors. She folded her laundry and put it away. In need of a break she sat back down at her computer to teach herself the mechanics of the dating website. When the screen came back up, she noticed that she had a response from Gram. It said, "No worries! I think this site has a mind of its own!! It puts ??? next to some of my statements I'll send a longer note soon! Enjoy your day!! ????" Oh how funny is that? Lynn thought. She quickly responded with, "I agree with the mind of its own, it won't let me change my birth date because I'm actually 35. I hope that's not a problem. My day is going well and I'm very grateful for the weekend. Talk soon." Gram was actually in her 50's but age was of no concern to Lynn, her attraction to women was based solely on their personality, followed by having a pleasant face to look at while in conversation. Lynn wouldn't hear from Gram for another three days and it was Lynn who reached out to her.

Lynn busied herself the rest of the day by cooking a big pot of soup. She loved soup and thought it to be soothing to the soul. She thought about making vegetable soup until she saw her bag of split peas in the pantry and quickly changed her mind, plus the protein would be good for her. She had some leftover Easter ham in the freezer; she took it out and placed it in the microwave to defrost. She decided that the Soup of the Day would be Split Pea and Ham. She checked her crisper and found a few carrots, celery, and onions. She rinsed her peas and placed them in the colander to drain; she diced her carrots in small chunks, and did the same with the celery and onions. If she was making vegetable soup, her chunks would be bigger. Hearing the microwave ding, she pulled her defrosted ham out and placed it on the cutting board. She chopped the ham into medium chunks because she liked ham and could eat just ham in one bite without any peas. It made her think of how one eats a sandwich: you eat the two corners and that leaves that one good bite right in the middle of the sandwich. She always considered a true friend to be a person who would give you the "good bite" of their sandwich. She wondered if Gram would give her the "good bite". She shook her head with the silly notion and continued making her soup. She put everything in her cast iron soup pot, filled it with water to just cover the mixture then added a quart of chicken broth, and placed it on the stove. She turned the burner to high to get the soup boiling before she lowered it to simmer. She salted and peppered it and stirred the pot; she would check her seasoning again later to see if she needed to add more. She turned and left the kitchen.

Lynn returned to her computer, she had brought some work home with her and thought that this was a good time to finish things that she wasn't able to accomplish because of her time being consumed with the return of the defective parts. She wrote a procedure on how to assemble the medium holder of a 3-D printer and began the outline for the new Quality Manual that incorporated the requirements of ISO 13485, Quality Standard for Medical Devices. Stan was insistent that the company become registered to this new standard. He claimed that it was the wave of the future and our destiny as a company was to be able to supply to the medical device industry. Lynn's thoughts didn't necessarily agree with Stan, especially after the large return. The quality of that product was deficient, and she just couldn't think about making parts that could possibly go inside the human body. It made her shudder. What if there was a failure in the field like at Hanscomb's? She wouldn't be able to live with herself if people had the potential to die on her watch.

She got up from her computer, went into the kitchen and turned the boiling soup down to simmer. It would have to simmer about 3 hours before it was ready which was ok with Lynn as it was only noon and she wasn't really hungry but she would be at dinner time. She liked eating dinner earlier on the weekends, during the week she didn't eat much dinner because she didn't want to go to bed with a full stomach, so a small salad or a half sandwich was enough to get her through until the next day. Lunch was usually her largest meal and even that was conservative. She covered the pot and went back to the living room and did some stretches. She remained limber but sitting for too long put pressure on her spine. She reached down and touched her toes, feeling her lower back elongate and stretch out. She stood upright, picked up the remote and clicked on the TV. She clicked on in time to start a movie about two people who met each other by chance and spent a day together in New York City. At the end of the day, he had written his phone number on a dollar bill and said, "Call me." She tossed the dollar up into the wind and said. "If that dollar comes back to me, then it is serendipity and we are meant to be together." Lynn fixed herself a cup of tea and settled in to watch and see if they found each other again. She was a sap for a good love story.

The love story went something like this; "During the Christmas season in New York City, Jonathan Trager encounters Sara Thomas at Bloomingdale's while they attempt to buy the same pair of black cashmere gloves. While they are both in relationships, a mutual attraction leads to sharing dessert at Serendipity, a small cafe. Sara reveals her opinion that fate determines many of her decisions in life. They encounter each other again when they both have to return to the restaurant to retrieve things that they had left behind. Considering this to be fate, they spend more time together and just after they exchange phone numbers Sara's gets blown into the wind. She interprets this as a bad omen so instead suggests alternative ways to put their numbers out into the universe.

She suggests that one put their name and phone number on a $5 bill and the other on the front endpaper of a book that will be sold the next day. If each finds the other's item they are meant to be together, and can make contact. Several years later, Jonathan is in New York City getting engaged to Halley Buchanan. On the same day, Sara is in San Francisco and comes home to find her boyfriend Lars Hammond proposing to her. Cold feet ensues as their respective wedding dates approach; they start their attempt to reconnect.

Sara flies to New York City and her friend Eve persuades her to give up the chase—they go to Serendipity. The $5 bill given to Eve in change has Jonathan's contact information. Jonathan gets as a gift from Halley on the night of the wedding rehearsal the same book that has Sara's phone number. He and his friend Dean fly to San Francisco to find her. Jonathan sees a woman at Sara's house who he thinks is Sara but is Sara's sister, Caroline, fooling around with her boyfriend. Jonathan believes that his chasing ghosts means that he does not want to marry Halley. On board a plane to return to San Francisco, Sara is buying a head set and finds that she has Eve's wallet with the $5 bill of Jonathan. She disembarks and makes her way to his apartment. His neighbors tell her about his wedding at the Waldorf Astoria where she discovers that his wedding has been called off.

Jonathan wanders Central Park, and comes upon a bench at the ice rink that has a jacket Sara had left behind earlier. He uses the jacket for a pillow while lying in the middle of the rink. He has with him one black cashmere glove. He gazes up at the falling snow and a cashmere glove falls on his chest. He sees it is Sara; the glove is hers. They introduce themselves to each other formally for the first time. In the final scene, Sara and Jonathan are at Bloomingdale's, enjoying champagne on their anniversary at the same spot where they first met."

It was serendipity, the faculty or phenomenon of finding valuable or agreeable things not sought for, as the movie ended, Lynn thought about the website and whether it would be serendipitous for her. Although she was more inclined to believe in fate, that which is something that happens to someone, than serendipity because she was used to charting her own course in life and not leaving her destiny up to the universe. She snapped off the TV, and thought about Gram and the website and wondered if it would be fate that brought them together; she returned to the kitchen to stir her soup. She sat back down at her computer to accomplish some more work and lo and behold, there was another message from Gram.

Chapter 10

"Gram"

Lynn's heart did that little skip when she saw the next contact from Gram. She ladled herself up a mug of soup and sat down at her computer to see what Gram had sent her. She blew on a spoonful of soup and opened the message. It read, "I'm so glad you responded to my message??? I'm very interested in meeting you??? Maybe we can get together for coffee sometime." Lynn did a double take and re-read the message again. "Oh my, she wants to meet me!" Lynn thought. Lynn jokingly responded, "I'm not doing anything tomorrow." Still not being totally familiar with the website, she was surprised when Gram immediately replied, "How about coffee, my treat." Oh wow, Gram was even willing to pick up the tab, too bad she didn't say dinner, Lynn chuckled to herself.

Gram lived about 40 miles away, just across the Vermont and Massachusetts state line and Lynn quickly searched the archives of her memory for a place that was half way in distance from her. She Googled the distance between them then selected a town that was around twenty miles from each other. She settled on Hudson, MA and remembered the quaint Main Street that ran through the town. She settled on a coffee shop called "The Bistro" and then returned to the dating website. She messaged Gram with the name and location and waited impatiently for a response. Within minutes, Gram responded with, "Great??? I'll see you there at two in the afternoon. I can't wait!" Lynn responded with, "I will see you there." Lynn could feel the first sign of butterflies in her stomach. To celebrate her new found love interest, she helped herself to another mug of soup and wrote another document.

Lynn put the soup in the fridge and scooped up three containers for lunch on Monday. She hoped the girls would like her soup so she was going to bring them their own serving. It's not good to share soup from one container. She went into her bedroom and stripped the bed of its sheet and threw them in the wash machine. She took clean sheets out of the linen closet and remade her bed. She loved clean sheets, especially after working in the yard all day and getting dirty. After her shower, her second best feeling was clean sheets next to her skin. She fluffed her pillows and placed the pillow shams in front of them along with her throw pillows. She retrieved her dusting supplies and dusted her bureau and head board. She silently gave herself grief because she should've dusted the headboard before she made the bed. Oh well, too late now, she thought.

She went into the bathroom and swept and mopped her bathroom tiled floor. She then scrubbed out the tub, shower, toilet, and vanity sink. She could check, "Clean bathroom" off of her list. Next, she went into the kitchen and did the same. She swept and mopped the floor, shook out the area rug, wiped off the stove top, and cleaned out the sink. She cleaned the countertops until they sparkled and then wiped off the appliances. Satisfied that the living spaces were cleaned, she made her way up the stair case to clean the second floor. She vacuumed the loft and the two bedrooms and swept and mopped the second bath. She didn't go up here much except when she wanted a bath. The second floor had a two person Jacuzzi tub and Lynn considered it her swimming pool. When her muscles were sore and extra tired, she would get in the Jacuzzi and let the jets massage her muscles.

Lynn descended the stairs, sweeping them off as she went. She put the dustpan under the pile that accumulated at the bottom of the stairs and swept it up. She dumped the contents in the trash and hung the dustpan and little broom on the hook in the basement stairwell. Now that the house was clean, she turned her attention back to her computer and thought about doing more work but when she sat down, she saw that she had received another message from Gram. She clicked on the little envelope and Gram's correspondence appeared. Lynn scanned the message and a frown creased her forehead, the message read, "Please wear something femme, I prefer a feminine touch." Lynn thought, "Hmmm, that is strange, what did she think I was going to wear?" This made Lynn a little anxious as to what to wear tomorrow. She never considered herself butch or manly; she was just cute in a sporty kind of way and wore clothes that were more preppy in style. She went to her closet and looked through her button downs and decided on the three quarter sleeve pink pinstripe. She next took out a pair of mid thigh white shorts from her bureau, a thin belt, and her Sperry Topsiders to complete the outfit. She decided that if Gram didn't like the way she dressed then maybe Gram wasn't the one for her. However, she remained hopeful that the encounter would be a success. She put on her night clothes, which consisted of a tee shirt and a pair of panties, brushed her teeth and climbed into bed.

Lynn awoke the next morning rather late and did her customary stretching, relishing this time when she could just be without an alarm blaring in her ear. She had been tired from riding her bike yesterday, then working for work, and then cleaning house. She then remembered that she had a date today and jumped out of bed with a start. She told herself to just calm down as she went to the bathroom to brush her teeth. She thought about going on a bike ride but thought better of it because she didn't want her legs budging from her shorts for her date and they always pumped up after riding her bike. She decided that she would kill time by going to the open air vegetable stand by her house to buy some fresh fruit and vegetables for the upcoming week. She threw on a pair of shorts, her bra, and a tee shirt, grabbed her purse, and went out to her Jeep. It was on the cool side so she went back in and took a hoodie out of the coat closet. She made a mental note to take a sweater with her when she went to meet Gram. She climbed into her Jeep, backed out of the drive, and drove to the fruit and vegetable stand. She parked, took out her recycled grocery bags and started toward the apples. She grabbed a basket, and in it, started placing apples, pears, and peaches. She then picked out a head of red leaf lettuce, some tomatoes, and a cucumber. She would make a salad for dinner this evening after her meeting with Gram. *Oh yes! Gram!* She was surprised that she had forgotten about the date and quickly looked at her watch. *Egads!* She needed to get going and start getting ready for her big date from the dating app. She paid for her produce and climbed back into her Jeep.

Lynn pulled into her driveway, took her groceries out, and entered her house. She put her fruit in the big fruit bowl on the counter and put the vegetables in the fridge. She folded her grocery bags and tucked them away and dropped her purse. She went to the bathroom and turned on the shower. She climbed in once she started seeing steam and began scrubbing her body and washing her short brown hair. She felt the butterflies again when she got out of the shower and dried off. She padded off to her bedroom and selected a white pair of panties because she was wearing white shorts after all. She decided a regular bra would be better than a sports bra and wondered why she was paying such close attention to the details unless she was trying to make a good impression and she had to admit to herself that she was. She slipped into her shorts and went back to the bathroom to apply her deodorant. She used men's deodorant because it kept her dryer and she liked the smell. She had tried women's deodorant, even the strongest one, and it didn't keep her dry. Besides, they all smelled like baby powder and that was one scent she particularly didn't care for, she preferred sporty and spicy scents. She went back to her bedroom, put on her button down, tucked it in, zipped up, and placed the belt around her waist. She went with a thin brown belt that matched her Topsiders, and then she slipped her feet into her shoes. She had only towel dried her hair so it was back into the bathroom for her blow dryer. She dried and styled her hair, applying just enough gel to give it volume. She put in small silver hoops in her ears, and placed a silver necklace around her neck. She chose her silver watch and wrapped it around her wrist and snapped the clasp shut. She went back to her closet and selected a maroon sweater, tied it around her neck, all the while letting most of the sweater hang down her back. She looked at her watch and thought if she leaved soon she would be there ten minutes early and that was socially acceptable.

Lynn picked up her purse again, opened and locked her door as she went out. She had a slight skip to her step as she made her way to her Jeep. She found herself backing out, driving down the bumpy drive, and turning toward the main road. She took the state Highway 119 to the Interstate I-495 and zoomed down the on ramp. She took her foot off of the accelerator and said to herself, "Whoa Cowgirl, you don't need to get stopped for speeding!" After 40 minutes, she took the exit for Hudson and turned right toward Main Street. She got lucky and found a parking spot right in front of the coffee shop, took one last look at her reflection in the visor vanity mirror, grabbed her purse, and stepped out of her Jeep. She smoothed out her shorts and walked to the door of "The Bistro". The butterflies were really fluttering now and she noticed her hand shaking a bit when she pushed open the door to the restaurant. She looked around at the tables, looking for one by the windows, and noticed that Gram was already here. She was sitting at a small table for two in front of the windows and smiled brightly at Lynn, waving at her. Lynn waved back and skirted the other tables, making her way to Gram.

When she arrived at the table, Gram immediately said, "You're late." This made Lynn look at her watch, thinking that she had misjudged the time for the ride, but her watch told her that she was ten minutes early.

She grinned at Gram and said, "I think I'm right on time, in fact, I'm ten minutes early even."

Gram responded with, "Proper etiquette is fifteen minutes early to any appointment."

Lynn responded with, "Oh, then I'm sorry for being late. Next time I will leave earlier."

Gram raised an eyebrow and stated, "If there is a next time."

"*Wow!*" Lynn thought, as she saw the smile turn into a grimace on Gram's face.

A waitress arrived at their table and grateful for the interruption, Lynn ordered a whole milk cappuccino while Gram ordered a Chai Tea.

Gram remarked, "Whole milk huh? I guess you don't need to watch your weight."

Lynn replied, "Well I do ride my bike everyday so I think that I can splurge every once in awhile."

Gram took in the comment and stated, "You are getting to an age where it will be harder to take off the pounds." Lynn had no reply.

To make conversation, Lynn asked if Gram was a shorter variation of another name, and Gram said, "Yes, it's short for Gramercy. I was named after my father, his name was Graham, and he was a wonderful man. He was very smart and earned his millions in seismology for oil companies."

Lynn guessed that this was supposed to impress her and she decided not to tell Gram that she hailed from the projects on the east side of Kansas City. Lynn quickly learned that Gram came from money and had lived a privileged life.

Their drinks arrived and each took a sip from their respective cups. Gramercy looked out the window and Lynn chose to no longer think of her as Gram because that name seemed gentler and kinder than the stuck up woman sitting in front of her.

Gramercy said, "I noticed that you drive a Jeep?"

Lynn smiled and said, "Yes, I do."

Gramercy added, "I had one of those in college but as I grew older I thought that I needed a more mature vehicle to drive."

Lynn thought, "*Oh great! Now my car is immature.*" She could hardly wait for the next insult so she quickly asked, "Really, what do you drive now?"

Gramercy half smiled and said, "See that Beemer parked in front of you?"

Lynn looked out the window and took in the sleek BMW convertible parked in front of her Jeep.

Lynn thought, *"And the hits just keep coming."*

Gramercy asked, "So, where did you go to college?"

Lynn was hesitant to answer because if it wasn't from an Ivy League school she was afraid that Gramercy would get up and walk out of the coffee shop. None-the-less, Lynn offered, "San Diego State University."

From the look on Gramercy's face, this was a mistake.

Gramercy scrunched her nose and said, "I was under the impression that you graduated from MIT since your profile stated you are a Mechanical Engineer."

Lynn replied, "I am a Mechanical Engineer, just not an MIT graduate."

Gramercy stated, "Oh that's a shame, MIT is a great school."

Lynn was getting really tired of Gramercy very quickly and she had only taken two sips from her cappuccino.

Gramercy inquired, "So what is your annual income? Because if it's not six figures than you are not working up to your potential."

Lynn was floored. She sat there shocked and thought to herself, "*Where does this woman get off asking me such a condescending question?*"

Lynn just shook her head and stated, "My boss thinks I am working up to my potential and that is the only opinion I care about."

"Oh, you have a boss? You don't report to the President or the owner of your little company?"

Lynn was getting aggravated and silently cursed this woman for lying on her profile. It said she was nice, and kind, and polite. Lynn determined that this woman was a Grade-A bitch and didn't deserve anything Lynn had to offer. In fact, Lynn thought that this woman was so rude and condescending that she could give Satan a run for his money.

Lynn decided to give Gramercy the benefit of the doubt and asked her if she volunteered to her community, spent time with the elderly, or gave to the homeless like her profile had proclaimed.

Gramercy said, "Oh no, I don't physically get involved with any of those indigent type programs, I just give them money. I have the income to do it and it's a great way to earn tax write offs. I find that more rewarding than actually rubbing elbows with the common folk."

Lynn couldn't believe what she was hearing; this woman was so self-absorbed that she couldn't get out of her own way! Lynn took another drink from her still warm coffee and thought it best to end this date. She placed her napkin on the table and motioned to the waitress to bring the check.

Gramercy raised her eyebrows and asked, "Are you leaving so soon? We just got here."

Lynn nodded and said, "Yes I'm leaving, although it was nice to meet you Gramercy, you are clearly too much for me."

Gramercy smiled her profile-winning smile and said, "I know what you mean, I get that a lot."

Lynn put a ten on the table and left the restaurant hoping to never see that woman again.

Lynn pulled out of her parking space and for a split second thought about clipping the Beemer's left rear bumper but thought better of it because she didn't want to hurt her immature Jeep. She cruised down Main Street Hudson, heading toward the Interstate that would take her back to her little humble cabin in the woods. She hit the four lane doing seventy miles an hour and took a moment to scream very loudly at no one. She just couldn't believe how some people could be so high and mighty. No wonder that woman was alone, who could be around her for more than ten minutes without wanting to punch her in the throat? Lynn silently fumed and made herself a promise to tell Jewel and Sabina that their dating website experiment was a big fat failure.

She exited off of the Interstate, made the loop onto Highway 119 as her heart sank, she was so hopeful that Gram would've turned out to be a woman that she enjoyed spending time with but that wasn't going to happen in this lifetime or the next.

Chapter 11

"With Friends Like This..."

Annie spent her weekend nurturing herself from her terrible date with Kelly. She felt bad that she just couldn't accept another person exactly for who they were, but she had such high hopes for her date and was severely disappointed when it turned out to be a disaster. Annie wanted to date someone, but she had her standards, and it wasn't like Kelly was sub standard, she just wasn't her type. Annie wanted someone who she found attractive. Ok, so maybe she was vane but she wanted to be happy with the package. However, the woman needed to have a good head on her shoulders and could carry on a conversation that didn't include "Little Missy". Speaking of "Little Missy" she had a few choice words to say to Maria tomorrow when she saw her at school.

Annie made her way into the kitchen to make her lunch for the next day. She didn't have cafeteria Proctor duty so she would brown bag it as usual. She pulled open her refrigerator door and peered inside as to the contents. She still had fruit and yogurt and stuff to make a salad with, so she took down a plastic container from the cabinet and made a small tossed salad that included lettuce, tomato, and radishes. She put the lid on the container and then pulled out an apple, an apricot, and a yogurt. She placed everything in her lunch bag and stuck the entire bag back in the fridge. She wrote on a sticky note, "Don't forget your lunch" and placed it on the front of her coffee maker. She often forgot her lunch but she never forgot to have coffee in the morning, and the sticky note always reminded her. She would take her lunch bag out in the morning and place it by her purse and book bag before she got in the shower, that way it would be right there with the rest of her luggage when she left the condo. It was still early on Sunday and she decided to catch something on TV before she went to bed.

Annie pushed the remote button and the TV sprang into life. She hit the guide button and scrolled through the shows that would be coming on within the next ten minutes. She read, "Survivor", nope, next show; Snapped, a show about how women snapped and usually killed someone, nope. Next. Serendipity, a movie about two people who meet by chance and connect, then they disconnect and live their lives, and then reconnect again. She liked both actors in the movie and maybe a love story with a happy ending is what she needed after the date from hell, so she popped some popcorn, opened a Diet Coke and settled in to watch the movie. She munched her popcorn, sipped her Coke, and found herself wishing she was Kate Beckinsale and that Kelly had been more like John Cusack. *That's it; maybe I need to go to New York City to meet Ms. Right because Albuquerque was not looking too promising at the moment.* She chuckled to herself and said, "Yeah right, that's really going to happen!" The movie ended, she was happy that they found each other, she turned off the TV and took her empty popcorn bowl and soda can into the kitchen. She rinsed out the can and placed it in the recycle bin. She washed out the bowl and placed it in the dish strainer. She then flipped the light off before going to the bathroom to floss and brush her teeth. She brushed her hair, washed her face, and walked to her bedroom, thinking about the movie and wondered, "*When? When is it going to happen for me?*" She tucked herself in alone.

Annie woke up the next morning to the sound of her alarm. She stretched and her feet hit the floor. This was going to be the day of reckoning for Miss Maria Gonzales. She did her morning routine of shower, blow dry, makeup on, dressed, and out the door. She had to go back in the condo to grab her lunch bag. She got to her car, stowed her gear, and backed out to go to school. She was on a mission to set Maria straight.

She made it to school in record time, parked in her usual spot and noticed that Maria's car was also there, which meant that Maria was in the building. She skipped the office and Miss Bea and went straight to the Teacher's Lounge where she was sure to find Maria. As soon as she walked in, Maria took one look at Annie and knew that the date didn't go well.

Annie just looked at Maria and said, "Are you new? Or don't you know me at all? What were you thinking about setting me up with Kelly? Haven't we talked about the type of women I am into? You should've known better or did you have too much sangria at that cookout of yours?" Annie didn't let up on the questions and Maria just sat there with her coffee cup paused in mid air, her eyes big, and her mouth open. Annie continued, "I can't believe that your cousin let you do this. He is a friend of mine and knows my likes and dislikes, or did you not even ask him his opinion before you decided to play

179

matchmaker? Really Maria, what were you thinking?"

Maria put her coffee cup on the table and meekly said, "I take it you didn't have a good time?"

Annie almost exploded, "A good time? Are you kidding? It was like being at a Tractor Pull in a Sushi Bar!"

Maria looked at Annie almost fearfully because she had never seen or heard Annie lose her temper. This outburst was so Un-Annie-Like that Maria was at a loss for words. All she could say was, "I am so sorry. Maybe the sangria did get the better of my judgment. But I thought for sure that you two would get along. Did you get along at all? Did Kelly say something that was offensive or rude?"

This last question made Annie stop her tirade and think about her date. She answered, "No she wasn't rude, she actually ordered for me but she ordered nothing of what I wanted. The only thing that was offensive was what she was wearing. Really Maria? A plaid sweater vest? In New Mexico? What kind of person wears that in

Albuquerque? And don't even get me started on her southern accent! Did you even talk to her before you offered me up?"

Maria frowned and said, "Now wait a minute. I thought her southern drawl was charming."

Annie countered, "Maybe if she was a plantation owner, but not if you want to make a good first impression."

Maria bowed her head and mumbled, "I'm so sorry! I will check with you first before I do this again."

Annie said, "Oh no, there will not be a next time. I've accepted my fate of being alone for a long time, especially if the only person I can get a date with is southern fried truck driver in a sweater vest."

Maria quickly interjected, "You know, you can always try one of those lesbian chat rooms."

With that being said, Annie groaned, turned on her heel, and left the Teacher's Lounge.

Maria looked at the other two teachers that were in the room who were standing there slacked jaw at what had just transpired and just said, "She's having a bad day."

One of the teachers said, "Really, I thought she was too pretty to be a lesbian."

The other teacher agreed, and said, "I know, but now I know why she wouldn't go out with me."

Maria just shook her head, rose from the table and went to the sink where she dumped her cold coffee down the drain.

As with Annie, Lynn woke that Monday morning ready to give Sabina and Jewel a piece of her mind about the types of people that frequented the Dating Website. She quickly showered, dressed, and left for work. She didn't even bother getting the three containers of split pea soup that she had set aside for her friends, which made her think to herself, *With friends like that, who needs enemies.*" She drove to work in silence and rehearsed what she was going to say to the Dynamic Duo. She parked her Jeep and wasted no time getting to her office. The normal people were lined up outside her door; the ever faithful Frank was there to say good morning. She put her hand up to all the guys and said, "Not today fellas, I have a bone to pick with a couple of ladies up front." She dropped her purse and briefcase and turned to leave without helping anyone in line.

Lynn found Jewel and Sabina in Jewel's office going over the latest accounting transactions. She stood in the doorway, her arms stretched across both door jambs and said, "Well, if it isn't the partners in crime." They both turned to look at her with big smiles on their faces but when Lynn raised that one eyebrow, their smiles faded.

Sabina was the first to talk and she asked, "Well, how did the date go?"

Lynn just shook her head and said, "It didn't go anywhere. It was a disaster!"

Jewel said, "Oh no, what happened? Your email said it looked promising."

Lynn replied, "I thought it was too, but you've obviously not tried cyber dating." Lynn explained how she and Gramercy met at the coffee shop and how it went downhill after she entered the restaurant.

Sabina asked, "How could that be. You hadn't even met her yet?"

Lynn told them that Gramercy thought the vehicle that she drove was immature and was ok for college but not for later in life.

Jewel asked, "What do you mean?"

Lynn said, "Well, as Gramercy put it: if I was not driving a BMW and earning six figures then I wasn't living and working up to my potential."

Sabina, trying to be supportive said, "Well she doesn't really know that you are a hard, and smart, worker."

Lynn shook her head again and said, "That wasn't the point that Gramercy was trying to make."

Sabina looked perplexed and asked, "Well if that wasn't the point, then what was the point?"

Lynn answered, "The point that she was trying to make was that she had money and the Beemer to prove that she was living and earning up to her potential. If one didn't possess certain materialistic items such as a BMW and a house on Beacon Hill, then they were unworthy of her presence."

Jewel looked horrified, "Well the audacity of some people! You should've had her call me; I would've lied about your salary."

Lynn gave a weak smile of gratitude and went on to tell them that Gramercy thought that she was a graduate of MIT because she was a Mechanical Engineer but when Lynn told her that she went to SDSU, well, that further lowered Gramercy's opinion of her. Lynn told both women that Gramercy reeked of money and that Lynn didn't bother telling her anything about her childhood or the dysfunctional family she grew up in.

Sabina piped up, "Don't you ever be ashamed of where you came from. It helped mold you into the kind, thoughtful person that you are today. Who cares about that woman anyway? There are more on that site and I'm sure you are going to find you one."

Lynn just stood there and shook her head and said, "I don't know if I'm going to pursue any more lunatics from that web site."

Sabina looked worried, "Oh but you have to, and you can't let one bad apple spoil the whole bunch."

Lynn replied, "Oh yes I can."

Jewel had an epiphany and said, "Why don't you go into one of those lesbian chat rooms? That way you don't have to actually meet anyone but you can get to know them."

Lynn looked at her incredulously, "What do you mean a lesbian chat room? Are you even listening to the words that are coming out of your mouth?"

Jewel looked perplexed, "What's wrong with a chat room? My niece went on one and met her fiancé. They are not all bad; you just need to find a good one." Lynn rolled her eyes, "Ugh! I wouldn't even know how to find one."

Sabina chimed in, "Oh I will show you, and it's really easy."

Jewel and Lynn looked at each other and once again decided not to broach that subject with Sabina. They both silently wondered how Sabina had gained such a vast knowledge of an alternative lifestyle. Before Lynn could rebuke the offer, Sabina pulled out her phone, punched the icon for the internet, and typed, "Lesbian chat room". A plethora of websites flooded her phone and Lynn leaned over her shoulder to have a better look.

Sabina scrolled down the page past the Ads and started reading off the names of gay and lesbian chat rooms. There was: "Talkwithstrangers.com", "Meetville.com", followed by "Chatstreet.com" and the list went on ad-infinitum. Sabina settled on "Chatstreet" and announced, "Oh look, we get to build you another profile."

"Oh no," thought Lynn, *"not another profile."* Before Lynn could protest, Sabina's fingers and thumbs were pounding out yet another version of Lynn's life. There was no need to ask questions, they already knew the answers. Lynn

had turned to talk to Jewel when Sabina lifted her phone and snapped a picture of Lynn.

Lynn frowned, "What was that for?"

Sabina replied, "You need a pic for your profile and they say that full body poses get more hits than just face shots. But wait a minute; I need another one of your face because there is room for two pictures. Sabina quickly snapped another picture of Lynn's face but unfortunately Lynn wasn't smiling.

Sabina said, "Come on! Smile, you doofus."

Lynn laughed at the silly name calling and Sabina took the photo. It came out great with Lynn looking like she was actually happy.

Lynn huffed and said, "I need to go to work but don't count on me for lunch. I'm going to ride my bike." And with that, Lynn turned on her heel and walked down the hall and through production to get back to her office. The line of people hadn't changed.

Chapter 12

"ChatStreet"

Lynn rode her bike at lunch that day, welcoming the sun on her face and the wind whistling through the gaps in her bike helmet. It was a beautiful day and she really hoped that spring had sprung. She liked the winter well enough but spring and fall were her favorite seasons because they were so similar. She loved the cool air, the leaves falling and then budding again after a cold winter. She was partial to pumpkin pie in the fall and potato salad in the spring. Potato salad was like the baton being passed from winter to spring. She didn't eat potato salad in the winter; she was more comfortable with soups, stews, and chowders. This reminded her that she had left the three containers of split pea soup in her fridge and felt bad because she left them at home instead of sharing the soup with

Sabina and Jewel. After all, she couldn't be mad at them, they were only trying to help.

The rest of the day went without incident and was comprised of the usual bickering between the inspectors. Jake tried to mediate as best he could but then would find himself smack dab in the middle of whatever conflict happened to be occurring at the moment. Lynn remained in her office sending emails here and there, re-writing the Quality Manual, and trying desperately to lower the stack of work that had piled up in just a week. She came to a good stopping place around 4:30 in the afternoon and decided it was time to call it a day. She powered down her PC, picked up her purse, switched off the light to her office, and walked toward the exit of the building to where she had parked her immature Jeep. She still couldn't get over that comment from Gramercy. She climbed into her Jeep and drove home.

After her tirade with Maria, Annie went to her classroom and did the same routine. She stood for a moment looking at the sun coming through the windows; she felt her heart begin to slow down. She turned on the overhead lights and walked over to Milton, he still had some food and water left so she was relieved that the janitor kept his word and took care of Milton before he went home. Integrity was very important to Annie and was always a characteristic that she searched for in other women. She thought that Lisa had integrity, at least until the end, and then her ability to keep her word fell just short of the mark. She went back to her desk and opened her book bag and took out the day's lesson plan, she didn't have time to prepare it on Friday because she needed to get ready for that God-Awful date.

The kids starting strolling into the classroom around 7:15, class started at 7:30. The lessons went exactly as planned with little or no interruptions until 11:30 when the first bell rang for lunch. Just as they had entered, the students strolled out of the classroom and headed toward the cafeteria. Annie waited until the last child had left the room then she stepped out into the hall and made her way to the Teacher's Lounge where she was sure she would run into Maria again. In a way, she was hoping that she would because she needed to apologize to her for the outburst this morning. The Lounge was empty when she entered; she skirted the two big tables in the middle of the room and opened the fridge to pull out her lunch bag. She sat down at the table, pulled the top off of her yogurt, and dipped in the spoon. She almost had the spoonful in her mouth when Maria walked through the door. She quickly put the spoon back in the container and said, "Maria, I want to apologize for my behavior this morning. I don't know what came over me but you didn't deserve the tongue lashing I gave you." Maria gently smiled and said, "It's okay, I forgave you before you left the room. Besides, you were right, I should've consulted with you before I opened my big mouth. It's just that I want only the best for you, and yeah, maybe Kelly wasn't the best, but it makes me sad to see you alone." Maria offered, "You can always try one of those dating app thingy's that is all the rage, or even a lesbian chat room. In fact, that may be the best route to take because you don't have to actually meet the person unless you want to. You can just chat and get to know one another." Annie sighed heavily and slowly shook her head at Maria. One thing you can say about Maria, she never gives up.

The rest of the day was spent crunching for the state scholastic exams. Annie knew that her kids were ready and would do great on the exams and would help bring the school up in passing percentages. Class ended with a one page essay as to why the students wanted to pass their exams. The last bell rang and the kids filed out one by one, tired from the grueling afternoon syllabus. Annie packed up her book case, took her purse from the bottom drawer of the desk, and started for the door; she turned the lights off on her way out. She walked to her Nissan, placed her bags in the passenger seat and rounded the car to the driver's side. Maria was leaving the building at the same time and yelled, "Don't forget, CHAT ROOM!" Annie climbed in her car, backed out of her space and drove to her condo.

Lynn rumbled up her driveway, cursing it once again for being like a washboard only with bigger peaks and valleys. She parked, took her bike off of the back and put it in the garage. She grabbed her purse and keys, and let herself into the house. She placed her purse and keys on the obligatory hooks and went to her bedroom to change into something a little more comfortable. She shed her clothes, tossed them in the hamper, and put on an old pair of gym shorts, a white vee neck tee shirt, a pair of booties, and her slippers. It felt so good to be out of confining clothes. She poured herself a glass of iced tea and walked toward the Great Room, she thought she might catch the evening news. As she walked through the dining area, she had to pass her desk and computer. She stopped, turned to her left and said out loud, "Oh why the hell not." Plus she was curious as to what Sabina had put in the chat room profile and wanted to make sure the pictures didn't show her with three heads and four eyeballs.

She typed in "Chatstreet.com" in the search engine and there it was, first on the list. She noticed that she had to log on but Sabina had not given her, her sign on credentials. She went and got her phone out of her purse and texted Sabina, "What is my username and password to Chatstreet?" Within thirty seconds, Sabina replied with, "Lynn1285" as the username and "IWANTTOBELOVED" as the password. Sabina then texted, "I'm so proud of you." Lynn felt ill. She sat back down at her computer and logged into the website. She found herself reading a screen that scrolled quicker than any human could possibly read. Some of the entries had little pictures by their screen names; others had little silhouettes, while a third had a cartoon type drawing of two women. She deduced that the pictures were actual people, the silhouettes were people who didn't have a picture posted, and the cartoon characters were "guests". She noticed her own picture in the upper right hand corner of the window and clicked on it. A drop down menu read, "My Profile" and "Logout". She clicked on "My Profile" to see what outrageous entries Sabina had made up. It read, "Don't sext me or ask me to role play. I won't be your slave because I would demand emancipation and the legal right to vote. If you want clean coherent conversation then I will gladly entertain your pm. I'm not looking for anyone and as of right now, no one is looking for me. So keep it decent and I will treat you with the same respect, courteousness, and honesty you bestow me. Peace out." Lynn was impressed. Sabina had set boundaries that she herself would've made and added a little humor. She liked it.

Annie pulled into her condo parking spot, turn off the ignition, and climbed out into the hot New Mexico sun, she was glad she wore another one piece shift dress, it was sleeveless and allowed for plenty of ventilation but she was still eager to get inside where it was cool and she could get out of the dress and ballet flats that adorned her feet. She leaned in and took her bags from the passenger seat, closed the door, and clicked the remote to lock the car. She made the short walk and climbed the stairs to her condo door. As soon as she opened the door she felt a cool rush of air surround her body. She hung up her keys and dropped her bags on the kitchen counter. She went to the bathroom and turned on the shower, unzipped her dress and wished again that there was someone there to do this for her; she dropped the dress, her panties and her bra on the floor and stepped into the shower. She rinsed her body and washed and rinsed her hair. She turned off the shower, took her towel off of the hook and began to dry off. She took another towel and wrapped her hair in the customary turban and padded into her bedroom. She slipped into a pair of running shorts and an old tee shirt from a 5k run that she participated in a few years back. She continued to towel dry her hair as she took both towels back to the bathroom to hang up. She brushed out her damp hair and washed her face one more time to make sure she removed all of her makeup. Still barefoot, she went into the kitchen and poured herself a large glass of ice water and sat down at her computer to check her personal mail.

She quickly deleted all of the spam that seemed to have made it passed her filters and then just sat there watching her screen saver fade in and out. Maria's last words haunted her, "CHAT ROOM". She went to her browser bar and typed in Lesbian Chat Rooms and hit enter. Her screen filled with website domains of women seeking women. At the bottom of the page the ticker indicated that there were seventy eight pages. Seventy Eight Pages! "Oh my Gosh, I will I ever get through this?" thought Annie. She double clicked the first one listed on the first page and discovered that it was an Ad, she backed out and scrolled down. The first real website was called "Chatstreet" and she double clicked on it. A registration window immediately opened up asking her to create a screen name and password. She thought a minute then typed in "AnniesNotHere" in the space provided for her screen name. She chuckled. Next, she created a password "westCOASTswing" she figured she would remember that but jotted it down anyway along with her username. She knew that she didn't want to post any pictures of herself because she was a teacher so she would stay signed in as a guest and filled out the section titled, "About Me". She typed in, "Single Femme, 5'7", blonde hair, hazel eyes…I'm a teacher so I won't post pictures but if we get to know each other we can share pics. I'm looking to make friends with people who can carry on intelligent conversations so if you are that person, hit me up."

Like Lynn, Annie sat reading a screened that scrolled way too fast for her to follow and there didn't seem to be a topic. People were just throwing things out there with LOL and LMAO tagged at the end. Annie crinkled her nose, "I don't find that funny" she thought. She sipped her ice water and read along when she saw this blue font type that stated, "Anyone up for a clean and decent chat?" She noticed that it came from someone named "Lynn1285". She also noticed that Lynn1285 had a picture by her screen name so she clicked on it an up popped Lynn's Profile. Annie read the profile and Lynn seemed genuine and sincere in her write up, unlike some of the other profiles she had read such as, "I like long walks on the beach with my girlfriend, until the LSD wears off and I realize I'm just dragging a stolen mannequin around a Wendy's parking lot." Although she found this humorous, Annie wasn't so sure she wanted to talk to someone who mentions LSD in their profile. She told herself, "If Lynn1285 comes back on, I will PM her." Sure enough, a few screen scrolls later, "Lynn1285" popped back up requesting another clean chat. Annie clicked on Lynn's picture and a Drop down Menu appeared with the first option being "Private". She clicked on it and a small window opened up with Lynn's picture in the upper left hand corner and a bubble at the bottom that said, "Type Something". Annie typed five words:

AnniesNotHere:
Hi, I like your profile.

Lynn was also watching the screen when she saw a little number 1 appear by the envelope on the Task Bar. She clicked on it and someone named AnniesNotHere sent her a private message. Lynn responded with:

Lynn1285:
Hello and thank you. How are you doing this evening?

Neither Annie nor Lynn was prepared as to where the chat room bubbles would take them. They would come to learn about each other, their likes, their dislikes; they would share intimate details and talk about a broad range of subjects. Through the fiber optic cable that ran from New England to New Mexico, two women would find themselves and each other. And so their first conversation went something like this:

AnniesNotHere:
I am doing well, thank you for asking.
Lynn1285:
You're welcome. So what brings you to the Asylum this evening?

AnniesNotHere:
LOL, the Asylum, that's funny. I'm new here, this is my first night. I'm just checking it out.
Lynn1285:
Me too, this is my first night but I can already tell by the conversations that I want to stay out of the main room. That place is scary!

AnniesNotHere:
I agree, I can't even keep up with it, it goes so fast. This is more my speed.
Lynn1285:

I'm not sure as to how to start so I will just ask questions and you can chime in when you feel like it. How does that sound?

AnniesNotHere:
That sounds great, but do you mind if I ask you questions back?
Lynn1285:
No, please do, I think it's the best way to get to know someone.

AnniesNotHere:
Thank you.
Lynn1285:
You're welcome

Both Lynn and Annie were impressed with how polite they were to each other. Maybe there is something to these chat rooms after all. Lynn began formulating questions for Annie.

Lynn1285:
Where are you from?
AnniesNotHere:
New Mexico and you?

Lynn1285:
New England, Massachusetts to be exact.
AnniesNotHere:
I hear that it's beautiful there.
Lynn1285:
It is, but so is the Land of Enchantment.
AnniesNotHere:
How old are you?

Lynn1285:
35. How old are you?
AnniesNotHere:
27.

Lynn1285:
What are some of the things you like to do for fun?
AnniesNotHere:
I like to dance, read, run, go shopping, and watch movies. What do you like to do?

Lynn1285:
I like to read, write, cook, build furniture, and ride my bike.
AnniesNotHere:
Oh that's great, we both like to exercise and read. But I'm not much of a cook and I surely can't build furniture. Lol

Lynn1285:
Lol. And I'm not much of a dancer unless you count me and my broom on a Saturday when I clean house. And I would rather take a beating than go shopping.
AnniesNotHere:
That's ok, you can carry my bags. LOL.

"Carry her bags?" Thought Lynn, well how cute is she. Annie's mind went to Lynn and bike riding; finally, someone who exercises. So far, they were both enjoying the conversation.

Lynn1285:
What do you do for work?
AnniesNotHere:
I'm a school teacher, it's in my profile. What do you do?

Lynn1285:
I'm a Mechanical Engineer, but I have worked as a Quality Manager for most of my career.
AnniesNotHere:
Oh really? Where did you go to school?

Lynn1285:
I went to San Diego State University. I was stationed there when I was in the Navy, so I went to school. Where did you go to school?

AnniesNotHere:

I went to Penn State. That is so cool that you were in the Navy. Thank you for your service.

Lynn1285:

Thank you. It was my honor to serve you. How did a graduate from Penn State end up in New Mexico?

AnniesNotHere:

I moved out here with my Mom when she divorced my Dad.

Lynn1285:

I'm sorry to hear about your parents, it's tough. My parents divorced too.

AnniesNotHere:

It was for the best. My Dad drank a lot so it wasn't a good place to be.

Lynn1285:

I know what you mean, my Dad was an alcoholic and he was a mean drunk.

AnniesNotHere:

It's amazing that we turned out as good as we did. I mean, I think you're a good person.

Lynn1285:

LOL. I am a good person. I try to always be kind. I get cranky, but even then, I can be kind.

AnniesNotHere:

Those are good qualities to have and are very rare these days.

Lynn and Annie continued to talk for two more hours, just asking questions, and getting to know each other. Both were caught up in the conversation without any predetermination as to how the chat would end. They felt like they could talk to one another for days and still not run out of things to talk about. At 11:00 Pm, Annie looked at the clock on her monitor and said:

AnniesNotHere:
Oh my, it's getting late and I have to teach in the morning.
Lynn1285:
Yes, I know. I have to get up early also. Maybe we should say goodnight?

AnniesNotHere:
Maybe we should, but I don't want to, I'm having a great time.
Lynn1285:
So do I, but maybe we can make a date to meet here tomorrow night and chat again.

AnniesNotHere:
I would like that very much. What is the time difference between us?
Lynn1285:
I think its two hours. Let me check. Yep, your two hours behind me.

AnniesNotHere:
I'm home by 5:00, is that too late for you?
Lynn1285:
No, it will only be 7:00 here, that's not too late for me, but don't you need to eat dinner?

AnniesNotHere:
I don't cook remember. LOL
Lynn1285:
That's right. LOL. So I will see online tomorrow at five your time. Thank you for a pleasant evening.

AnniesNotHere:
You got it. Rest well and thank you.

With that, both Lynn and Annie logged off of ChatStreet feeling a little lighter, a little happier. Even though they had no idea what each other looked like, they were able to connect without the awkwardness of appearances. They could both be as ugly as mud fences but that didn't even cross their minds. What they felt was the ability to experience another human being without the pretenses of judgment or bias. They just enjoyed talking to one another, even if it was through the internet.

Chapter 13

"Getting to Know You"

Lynn woke the next morning before her alarm went off. She stretched like she always does but this morning; she looked up at the ceiling and smiled. She felt contentment but couldn't explain why. It was just a conversation with a screen name in a chat room, so why did she feel this magnetic pull from the universe telling her that this is more than just talking to someone. For the first time in a long time, Lynn couldn't figure out what she was feeling, she just knew that it wasn't a bad or negative feeling. It was surreal. That is the only term that came close to describing the lightness that she felt in her heart. She needed to slow down and get a grip on her feelings. This just wasn't supposed to be happening after one encounter and hell, she didn't even know if the person on the other end of the fiber optic cable was even a woman. However, right now, standing in the kitchen of her cabin in the woods, she felt hope. She made her coffee, she didn't get the pot ready the night before like she always does and then she remembered what she was doing last night. She had met a person in a chat room and lost all track of time and chores.

Lynn took a shower while her coffee was brewing. She went into her bedroom closet and selected a pink and white checked button down shirt, a pair of wrangler jeans, and her maroon work shoes. She dressed quickly and went to get her coffee before she went into the bathroom to finish her prep work. She brushed her teeth and brushed her hair, and then she took a sip of coffee and wrinkled her nose at the taste of her toothpaste mixed with coffee. She smiled in spite of the taste. She wondered if anything could bring her down today. She fixed her to go cup and went to put her bike on her Jeep, she was going to have a good ride today, and she could already feel it. An old song by Katrina and the Waves popped into her brain, "Walking on Sunshine" and that is what she felt. She felt like she was walking on sunshine. She secured her bike to the back of the Jeep then went back inside to get her coffee, purse, and keys. She locked the door on her way out as she skipped down the three steps of her deck. When she got to her Jeep she remembered that she wanted to take split pea soup to the girls, they were deserving of the food offering, it was their idea to go into the chat room. She rushed back inside and pulled the containers out of the fridge and resumed her trip back to the Jeep.

Annie didn't wake up before her alarm but did wake up with a smile on her face. She put her arms above her head and stretched and then giggled. Normally so serious, she was grinning. She laid there for a few minutes, basking in the warmth that ran through her body. She giggled again and thought, "Jesus Annie, it was just a conversation in a chat room." In her mind's eye she created a vision of what she thought Lynn might look like, she had no clue and Lynn's face took on a persona of other people that she knew so she really couldn't wrap her brain around an image. Her feet hit the floor and she reached her arms in the air and finished her stretch. She felt good. She went to the kitchen and put a pod in her Kuerig and punched the "brew" button. She lifted her fingers to her chin and strummed as she contemplated this evening's soon to be chat. She had a moment of panic and thought, "Oh no, what if she doesn't show up?" She quickly rid that thought from her mind and went back to daydreaming about how 5:00 couldn't come quick enough. She caught herself and said aloud, "Annie, you are just being silly. It wasn't that big of a deal." However, her heart said, "Yes, this was a big deal."

Annie took her cup of coffee and headed to the bathroom to shower and brush her teeth and begin her day. It was going to be another hot day so the uniform of the day would be a cotton skirt and a linen blouse and a pair of sandals that matched the color of the skirt. She dried her hair, applied her makeup, dabbed some cologne behind her ears and on her wrists, and then touched everything off with a set of sapphire earrings that matched her blouse. She picked up her coffee cup and went back to the kitchen. She dumped the remainder down the drain, rinsed out the mug, and placed it in the dish strainer. She picked up her bags, took her keys off of the hook, and headed out the door. She drove to school listening to one of her favorite cd's, humming all of the way.

The day seemed to drag for both Annie and Lynn, except when they found themselves thinking about their virtual date that would occur from two different points in the country; one from the East Coast and one from the West Coast. The day would prove to be longer for Lynn; she had to endure the time difference and decided that she would ride her bike after work instead of at lunch. It would make the time pass quicker until she needed to be online at 7:00 Pm. At precisely 5:00, Annie logged onto the website as did Lynn. They both could tell the other was in the chat room because their names appeared in the right hand column called "The Friend's Wall". Lynn made contact first by clicking on Annie's "Guest" icon and said:

Lynn1285:
Good evening, how are you? It's good to see you.
AnniesNotHere:
OMG, you actually showed up! I'm so glad, I'm doing better now.

Lynn1285:
LOL. Well I'm glad you are doing better, were you doing worse?
AnniesNotHere:
No, I just meant that I am doing better now that you're here.

Lynn1285:
Were you waiting long?
AnniesNotHere:
To be honest, I logged on here early so I would make sure to see you.

Lynn1285:
Oh my, a little anxious are we?
AnniesNotHere:
Yes, I'm anxious, aren't you?

Lynn1285:
A little bit, (lol) it's just crazy.
AnniesNotHere:
I know, I couldn't believe how long the day was, all I could think about was logging on and talking to you.

Lynn1285:
Yes, the day seemed interminable.
AnniesNotHere:
So, what would you like to talk about?

AnniesNotHere:
You start. Lol
Lynn1285:
Ok, What do you consider your best personality trait?
AnniesNotHere:
Oh that's an easy one, my honesty. I'm very honest, what's yours?
Lynn1285:
My integrity, I always keep my word. Good, bad, or indifferent

AnniesNotHere:
What do you consider your best physical asset?

Lynn1285:
Hmm, it would have to be my eyes. My eyes are blue and they change color with my mood. If I'm upset, they are darker. If I'm tired they are lighter. What is yours?
AnniesNotHere:
Definitely my legs, I love to dance and I have dancer's legs.

Lynn1285:
What do you consider your greatest achievement?
AnniesNotHere:
Becoming a teacher and paying off my student loans without any help from my Mom. What is your greatest achievement?
Lynn1285:
I've been published. I wrote a Technical Paper on Quality Circles and it was published in a magazine.

AnniesNotHere:
That is so cool! I'm in the presence of a famous writer. Lol

Lynn1285:
Well, I'm not famous but I can write. What is your favorite food?

AnniesNotHere:
Well it used to be sushi but I had a bad experience the last time I had sushi so I will say tacos.

Lynn1285:
What happened the last time you ate sushi? Did you get sick?

AnniesNotHere:
Let's just say that I had to leave the restaurant in a hurry. How tall are you?

Lynn1285:
I'm a stately 5 foot 4 inches. Lol. How tall are you?

AnniesNotHere:
I'm 5'7" and weigh 125.

Lynn1285:
Well, I didn't ask you your weight but we'll go with it. lol
Who is your favorite Author?

AnniesNotHere:
Michael Connelly, I love a good mystery. Who's yours?

Lynn1285:
That would by Hemingway. I still sob every time I read A Farewell to Arms. What is your favorite flower?

AnniesNotHere:
Hand's down, the Calla Lily.

AnniesNotHere:
How long was your longest relationship?

Lynn1285:
Eight years. And yours?

AnniesNotHere:

Only one year, I mean I had girlfriends in college but nothing serious until Lisa.

Lynn1285:
What happened?
AnniesNotHere:
I'm still not real sure as to what happened. She came home one day, said she was tired of the relationship, packed her things, mostly clothes, and left. I was devastated.

Lynn1285:
I'm sorry that happened to you.
AnniesNotHere:
So am I because I think it made me a little bitter. In fact, I know it made me bitter and reluctant to get back out into the dating scene.

Lynn1285:
Well, maybe we can work at turning that around for you and get you back out there and available.
AnniesNotHere:
I don't know if I want to get back out there. I kind of like it right here with you.
Lynn1285:
I'm glad because I like being here with you. It's very comfortable talking to you.

AnniesNotHere:
I know, isn't it strange? This is only the second time we've chatted but I feel like I've known you for a lifetime. Do you think that's weird?

Lynn1285:
I don't think that's weird, maybe a little accelerated, but definitely not weird. Weird would be wanting to go on a date after only talking to each other twice and living half way across the country. That would be borderline stalking. You're not a stalker are you? lol

AnniesNotHere:
No, I don't think I'm a stalker, but sometimes desperate means require desperate measures. Lol. All joking aside, I like to think of myself as somewhat normal. How about you? Are you normal?

Lynn1285:
Yeah, and my first name is Abby. Lol

AnniesNotHere:
Really? I thought your first name was Lynn.

Lynn1285:
LMAO, by chance you wouldn't happen to be blonde would you?

AnniesNotHere:

As a matter of fact, I am a blonde. Why do you ask?

Lynn1285:

(Lynn smiled that Annie didn't get the joke) No reason really, I just thought it was my turn to ask a question.

AnniesNotHere:

Oh that's right, we were playing the question and answer game. I have a question; How often do you ride your bike and how far?

Lynn1285:

Technically that is two questions but I will answer both. I try to ride my everyday and the mileage is dependent on how much time I have. If I'm riding at lunch, I only get to ride about 15 miles, but if it's the weekend, I can stretch it out to 25 or 30 miles.

AnniesNotHere:

Oh wow, and I thought I was doing well with my three mile runs, you must be really toned.

Lynn1285:

I don't know about being toned but I've been told I have nice legs. Why do you ask?

AnniesNotHere:

Well, I've heard that some bike riders develop really big thighs from riding their bike. Do you have really big thighs?

Lynn1285:
LOL, I don't know if I would tell you if I did, but no, my thighs are proportionate to my body. You ask strange questions at times.

AnniesNotHere:
I'm a visual person and I'm just trying to get a visual image of you in my head.

Lynn1285:
Well why don't you just ask me for a picture? LOL

AnniesNotHere:
You mean you would send me a picture? I don't think we can do that on this website. How would I get it?

Lynn1285:
From what I've learned, you can't send pics on this site but if you give me your email address, I can send you one.

AnniesNotHere:
That would be great, and I will send you one of me.

Annie sent Lynn her email address and Lynn scrolled through her photos to pick out two pictures that she thought Annie would like. She opened her own email, typed in Annie's email address and attached a photo of herself with her bike and a picture of when she was getting an award in the Navy. They both showed her face and profile. She typed a short, "Here ya go." and hit the Send button. She went back to the chat room and told Annie that she had mail. Annie responded with a "brb" which was an abbreviation for Be Right Back. For being new to chat rooms, Annie was picking up the lingo very quickly. Lynn made a mental note to ask Annie about that. After a few minutes, Annie came back to the chat room and said, "OMG, you are so cute!" Lynn chuckled and asked for Annie's picture in return. Annie responded with, "You have mail." Lynn typed in the obligatory "brb" and went back to her email account. She opened the email from Annie and she had left a message that said, "I hope you like it." Lynn hesitated a moment before she opened the picture. She had thoughts of doubts, "What if Annie was unattractive?" Lynn had created her own image of Annie and of course, she was striking in her mind's eye. Lynn moved the mouse over the attachment, closed her eyes, and double clicked. When she opened her eyes she was looking at a gorgeous woman wearing a blue dress. Lynn caught her breath and immediately thought, "Why is this woman in a chat room? Annie was beautiful and should have no problem finding a date, but here she was, talking to Lynn. Lynn's next thought was, "Well their loss is my gain." Lynn caught herself and said out loud, "Girl, you just met this woman and you have already claimed her as your own!" Lynn had to calm herself down. She returned to the chat room and Annie had left several messages while Lynn was away.

AnniesNotHere:
What do you think?
AnniesNotHere:
You hate it don't you?
AnniesNotHere:
Why are you taking so long?
AnniesNotHere:
Are you there? Did you leave?

Lynn came back to the chat room and said, "I am here." Annie immediately responded with, "It's not a very good picture is it?" Lynn replied, "On the contrary, you're beautiful."

Chapter 14

"Shared Secrets"

Lynn and Annie continued to talk until it was late and both of them agreed that it was probably time to sign off again, even though neither one was inclined to do so. They just kept saying good night pleasantries until Lynn shut her side of the site down. Lynn and Annie spent the next months, chatting and emailing. Most of their conversations were light in nature but sometimes they took a turn toward darker subjects. Especially when they spoke of their fathers and how they used to drink. They talked about almost anything and everything from how their day was to how they liked their coffee. They shared their goals, hopes, and dreams with one another. They continued with Quid Pro Quo and learned that one of them liked mustard and ketchup on their hamburger while the other one preferred mayonnaise. They also shared as many pictures as they could.

Lynn took pictures of her cabin and Annie took pictures of her condo in return. They showed each other their latest hair styles and wanted each other's opinion on outfits. They shared intimate details on what they thought their perfect date would be; what a romantic night at home would entail; and if they would ever marry someone. Lynn stated that she would never marry whereas Annie would love to marry. Lynn talked about buying a new bike. Annie asked how much it would cost, and when Lynn told her three thousand dollars, Annie told her she needed mental help because who in their right mind would spend three thousand dollars on a bicycle. Lynn countered with, "But it's a Cannondale; it's like the Ferrari of bicycles!" Annie replied, "Then buy a Ferrari!" They both laughed.

Annie told Lynn that she was attending a Dance Convention in Santa Fe and that she wouldn't be able to chat the next weekend. Lynn inquired as to what a Dance Convention was and Annie almost lost her mind with surprise. How could anyone not know about Dance Conventions?

Lynn replied, "Maybe people who don't dance."

Annie made a comment like, "Well we're just going to have to fix that!" Lynn wondered what that meant but decided not to pursue the statement lest she ended up at some Dancing

Convention that she had no plans of attending. Besides, New Mexico was a long way from Massachusetts. Which made Lynn think, "How far was this online thing going to go?" She put the thought out of her head and decided to just enjoy Annie for the moment but she wondered if she could prevent her feelings from developing for this gorgeous blonde elementary school teacher in New Mexico? She had no clue if the feelings were being reciprocated and decided to ask Annie;

Lynn1285:
I've been meaning to ask you, what do you think of our time spent together in the chat room?
AnniesNotHere:
Oh I think it's wonderful. We have a lot in common but are different enough to keep each other interested.

Lynn1285:
Yes, this is true, we do have many things in common and we have shared a lot of things, some of those things were superficial while other topics were deeper and more intimate.
AnniesNotHere:
I agree that random topics have been our way of getting to know one another, and there have been

topics that were deeper in thought. As far as intimacy goes, we can only be as intimate as this chat room will allow us to be. But I like you and want to spend as much time with you as possible even though there are thousands of miles between us.

Annie's last sentence pleased Lynn, she had said it, and the feelings were mutual. Or at least that is what Lynn read into the statement. However, without being in each other's presence and having a face to face conversation, it still left room for doubt. Lynn knew how she felt, and if the truth be known, she had a major league crush on Miss Annie, but did Miss Annie have a crush on her. She still wasn't convinced that Annie knew how she felt but thought it was the right time to chat about it. She wanted to share her secret before Annie went to the Dance Convention the next weekend. So she told Annie;

Lynn1285:
I like you too. I mean really like you and would like to take this virtual relationship a little further.

There was a long pause and Lynn counted off the minutes waiting for Annie to reply. And the longer she waited, the more nervous she became.

AnniesNotHere:
Lynn, I don't know what to say to that, how far can this relationship (if that's what you want to call it) go because we live in two different states. It's not like we can jump in our cars and meet up somewhere for coffee.

Lynn read the screen and became concerned that she had crossed a boundary that Annie wasn't yet ready to cross. She had misinterpreted what Annie had said about wanting to spend as much time with her as possible, but it was "virtual" time. Neither had mentioned actually meeting in real life, even though Lynn had the money and the time, to be on a plane to Albuquerque in a New York minute, she never mentioned it to Annie. She was hoping that Annie would be the first to approach that subject. Lynn didn't like the direction the conversation was heading so she quickly chatted;

225

Lynn1285:

I was just having a moment and wanted to share that with you. No worries, we can just be virtual friends, forget I said anything.

AnniesNotHere:

Ok good, because I just don't see how anything permanent or real can come out of this online friendship. We live totally different lives; you are there and I am here, and even though I have had those types of thoughts about you, I push them aside in order to not get too deeply involved and be hurt in the process.

Lynn1285:

Like I said, I was just having a moment, no big deal. Let's put it behind us.

AnniesNotHere:

No, it was important enough to you to want to tell me. I'm just having reservations about how deep to let myself fall, because I could easily fall for you but the practical side of me knows that it would be nearly impossible for us to have a real relationship.

Lynn1285:
It's really ok, I understand, forget about anything I said about it, and let's change the subject. How's the weather there?

AnniesNotHere:
The weather, why do you want to know about the weather?

Lynn1285:
Lynn had to chuckle and said out loud, "I wonder if she knows how adorable she is?" She typed, "The weather comment was just a way to change the subject."

AnniesNotHere:
Oh, ok. Lol
Lynn1285:
So, what would you like to talk about?

AnniesNotHere:
Well, it is getting late and I have papers that I still need to grade, can we chat another time?
Lynn1285:
Oh yes, I don't want to keep you, we can chat again later.

AnniesNotHere:
HAGN (Have a Good Night)
Lynn1285:
Good night

As soon as she saw Annie leave the room, Lynn knew that something had changed between them. The feeling in her stomach told her that it wasn't just a misinterpretation of a few words on the screen. This was a big FUBAR (Fucked Up Beyond All Repair) and she wondered if their time together in the future would be the same. Lynn knew that she probably blew it with Annie by pushing the "feelings" envelope. It was a shortcoming that Lynn needed to work on, but they had been communicating for months and the feelings just kept getting stronger with every keystroke from her computer. It's not that she obsessed over Annie; Lynn was independent enough to carry on smartly in her life. She still went to work every day and gave it her all. She still rode her bike daily and performed all of the activities of daily living. She coordinated the repair of the big return from Hanscomb's and was eventually able to return the entire product to them and they were grateful. So was Stan, he was glad that they didn't have to scrap thousands of dollars. Even Derek was impressed as to how she handled the rework of the little defective parts. It took a lot of coordination with the Engineering Department to get it just right, but they prevailed.

Lynn thought about Annie every day. Sometimes the thoughts were just snippets of memories when she heard something that Annie may have said, other times she would let her mind spend more time with Annie, especially when she rode her bike. She would plug herself into her Mp3 player and ride for a long time, listening to sappy love songs and wondering what Annie was either doing or thinking. She would go home every night, turn on her computer, and look to see if there was a number by the little envelope that indicated that someone had left her a message. She would sit and read the scrolling screen and wait to see if Annie showed up but after five days, with two of those days being a very long weekend that found Lynn washing and waxing her Jeep even when it didn't need it but it killed four hours of her time and exhausted her enough to put her to bed early. She scrubbed her deck and put another coat of stain on it because it took a beating last winter. She cleaned out her basement and separated things between donations and throw away. She organized her pantry and ironed all of her button down shirts. She did a lot of things that she had put off since encountering Annie, but to be honest, she just did these things so that she wouldn't think about Annie and how she missed talking to her. She felt like something was missing, or that she had misplaced her keys, or forgot why she came into a room. There was a small space in her heart that Annie occupied and now that space was empty and Lynn would find herself sad at times. After a month of moping around, Lynn decided that the most cathartic thing she could do would be to write. She had always kept a journal, and would jot down thoughts, goals, dreams, how her day was, and sometimes, just what she had for dinner. She returned to her journal and began pouring out her thoughts and emotions. Little did Lynn know that when she clicked off on the last night that she chatted with her, that she wouldn't hear from Annie again. Lynn stopped going into the chat room.

Annie was going through her own stages of grief with the loss of Lynn. She knew that she should contact her and that it was rude to just fall off the face of the earth like that, but she just couldn't bring herself to turn on her computer for anything other than work. It scared Annie when

Lynn shared her feelings with her, and she so much wanted to share her feelings with Lynn but didn't have the courage to face rejection or the possibility of pain. As much as she cared for Lynn, Annie was too guarded to throw her inhibitions to the wind and just "Go for it". For every reason that she thought that it could work with Lynn, there were at least three reasons she thought of as to why it wouldn't work. Annie honestly thought that this was her way of justifying why she left the chat room and Lynn. She was confused and scared. How can a person care so deeply for someone that they have never met or even talked to on the phone, because they never exchanged phone numbers. She knew that if she ever heard Lynn's voice she wouldn't be able to help herself and the slight fall that she would have would turn into a full blown header and she would be hopelessly lost and in love. So she wouldn't let herself go there. Instead, she would cry herself to sleep. Her fear of the pain of losing someone again was much greater than her fear of being alone.

Chapter 15

"The Teacher and The Squid"

Lynn spent the following months trying to write Annie out of her system. She filled two journals with pages of sadness, anger, joy, denial, and loss. At the end of three months of pouring her thoughts, hopes, dreams, and pain onto paper she decided that the best way to pay homage to her time with Annie was to write a book. She had always wanted to write a book but never found the time or the motivation to put pen to paper. She had written manuals, policies, and procedures but never anything personal, or especially anything that remotely had to do with love. That subject was totally out of her wheelhouse. However, she was compelled to write and the story of The Teacher and The Squid was born. Annie was of course the teacher and Lynn was the squid, a nickname bestowed upon Navy sailors. Her feelings, even if they were played out in a virtual environment, needed to be honored. So she wrote. She wrote truths and she wrote about stories that they shared like the time Lynn took Annie on a scavenger hunt in the chat room. Annie sat and read as Lynn told her a story of her hypothetical birthday.

In this story, Lynn had Annie drive to different locations such as a coffee shop where she would get a coffee and an envelope that would lead her to her next destination. Lynn typed this entire story out in the chat room and Annie read as Lynn typed. The story ended with Annie sitting on a park bench and the card in the envelope said, "Hello my love, I hope you enjoyed your birthday jaunt. You are more deserving than just a dinner and a gift, so I took you on an adventure. Now turn around." Annie turned on the bench and there stood Lynn with a bouquet of Calla Lilies and a ring asking Annie to marry her. This was one of many stories that Lynn would write in her book.

Another story took place at a ski resort in Red River, New Mexico where they went to dinner and danced to Pachelbel in Canon D. On their way back to their cabin, they stopped to look up at the stars and Annie's beauty was accentuated by the full moon and Lynn fell in love all over again. In every fictitious story that Lynn wrote in the book, Annie was with her in person. They went to places like Vancouver, British Columbia and walked the rocky beaches. They traveled and they loved each other fiercely and with much passion. They were truly soul mates and in Lynn's book, they lived happily ever after, but in real life, it was merely Lynn's way of purging herself of her feelings.

Lynn stumbled upon a lady in the chat room that acted as her editor. After every chapter, Lynn would email it to "Duckii" and Duckii would edit what Lynn had written. Duckii would reformat the paragraphs, punctuate the dialogue correctly, and make recommendations. Lynn grew to trust the Duck and always valued her opinions. Plus the Duck loved the book and that pleased Lynn immensely. In fact, she dedicated the book to the Duck. She had grown to like the Duck, and they texted each other on a daily basis just to check in and see how the other one was doing. Another virtual relationship developed and Lynn considered the Duck to be her friend and editor. Duck kept telling Lynn that she needed to find a "real" editor but Lynn was happy with her Duck so she dismissed her suggestions.

At the end of the book, Lynn printed a rough draft and took it to work for Sabina and Jewel to read. They both enjoyed the book and told Lynn that if she didn't have it published she was stupid. Lynn never thought about it being published, she just wanted to write a book and then she could mark that off of her bucket list. Besides, the whole intent of writing the book was to get over Annie, and for the most part it worked. Lynn could make it through the day without feeling that emptiness in her heart and the void in her mind that Annie used to occupy.

Unbeknownst to Lynn, she was unaware of Jewel's connections. Jewel made a copy of Lynn's book and sent it to a publisher friend. Time passed and Lynn went on about her days and nights; it was back to business as usual until one day when Lynn received a phone call from Jewel. Jewel needed to see her in her office and that she had good news to share. Lynn entered Jewel's office and there was a man that Lynn had never met, sitting across from Jewel.

He rose to shake Lynn's hand and said, "Hi, I'm John Wilkins and I'm a friend of Jewel's."

Lynn shook his hand and said, "Hello, it's nice to meet you. Any friend of Jewel's is a friend of mine. How can I help you?"

John sat back down and said, "It's not what you can do for me but what I can do for you."

Lynn raised her eyebrows and said, "Oh really? I didn't know that I was in need of help but ok, I'll bite."

John pulled out a business card from the breast pocket of his suit jacket and handed it to Lynn. Lynn read the card; it said, "John Wilkins, Editor & Publisher", "Small Time Press". Lynn looked perplexed and John continued, "Jewel here sent me a draft copy of a book titled, "The Teacher and The Squid" and I was impressed and wanted to meet the author and offer my services to publish your book."

Lynn was still trying to wrap her brain around the idea of her book being published when John kept saying things such as, "We'll need to get artwork for the cover, and my firm can handle that. As far as marketing goes, you will have all say in the matter, but we can offer some locations where your book will get exposure and of course we will have an e-book."

Lynn looked at Jewel and asked, "Is this guy for real?"

Jewel answered, "I assure you he is the real deal."

John went on to say, "I'm thinking that we'll print a couple thousand paperback issues and around 100 hardbacks, authors are funny that way, they don't think they are writers until they see their work in a hardback edition, and of course there is the book signing tour."

Lynn's face was blank, this was so surreal and beyond her comprehension. John leaned over and picked his briefcase up off of the floor and clicked it open. He withdrew a stack of papers that Lynn needed to sign in order to get her book printed.

Lynn finally came out of her somewhat fugue state and asked, "Can I have a moment to read this before I sign it?"

John agreed, "Oh yes, take your time, take it home with you and read it overnight and get back to me tomorrow."

John stood up, shook Lynn's hand again, then turned to Jewel and said, "Thank you so much for this gem; I have a good feeling about this."

Jewel thanked John for coming in and then escorted him to the front door of the building.

Jewel rushed back down the hall to Lynn and grabbed her by the arms and shook her, saying, "Oh My God, can you believe it? You are going to be a published writer! I knew this would happen as soon as I read your book so I just had to call John and get him involved. I hope you don't mind."

Lynn shook her head, "No I don't mind, but is he for real? Does he really want to publish my book?"

Jewel nodded like a bobble head and said, "He most certainly does, I told you it was a good book."

That evening Lynn found herself reading over the publishing contract. Everything was detailed. The size of the book, the number of pages, the dust jacket and paperback art work, a list of book stores that would carry the book, and of course, the marketing aspect of it. Then there was the e-book version to be sold on Amazon and BookBub. Lynn read the contract three times and couldn't find any loopholes, even in the fine print at the bottom of the last page. Everything seemed in order, so she grabbed a pen, signed the contract, and placed it in her purse. She would call John in the morning to come and pick it up or she could take it to his offices at the publishing house at lunch time. She decided on the latter because she wanted to make sure that "Small Time Press" was a legitimate business. She didn't doubt Jewel, Lynn just wanted to see for herself.

Around 9:00 the following morning, Lynn called John, told him that she had signed the contract, and would be dropping it off at his office around 12:30. John said that was great and he looked forward to seeing her again. At noon, Lynn drove her Jeep to the location of Small Time Press as shown on her phone GPS. She parked her Jeep in the parking lot and walked through the front door of a little company that would prove to change her life for the better.

She told the Receptionist that she was there to see John Wilkins and the lady behind the big counter said, "Oh yes, he's expecting you."

The Receptionist picked up her phone and dialed John's office and told him that Lynn was there to see him. As Lynn waited, she looked around the neat waiting room and noticed a small placard with detachable letters, it said, "Welcome, Lynn Tunney, Our Newest Author."

Even though it was a small sign, it gave Lynn butterflies to read her name along with the word "Author". She never considered herself an author, a writer maybe on a good day, but never an author. John came down the hall from his office to the waiting room and pumped Lynn's hand up and down in an excited motion and again, thanked her for allowing Small Time Press to publish her book.

Lynn said, "The gratitude is all mine."

They went back down the hall that John just emerged from and went into his office. John Wilkins's office looked like a small library. There were floor to ceiling book cases full of books, stacks of books on the floor, and on his desk. Along with draft copies of other books that he was reviewing. Lynn asked him how the screening process was going, and he said it was ok, but none of the people in that stack had the talent that Lynn possessed.

Lynn blushed at the compliment and said, "I'm sorry, I'm still getting used to this whole idea."

John said, "No problem, before you know it, you'll be writing another book and I will be hounding you to finish it." John asked her if she wanted something to drink and she graciously declined. She sat in the only chair that didn't contain any books, and pulled the signed contract out of her purse. She had flagged some pages that she wanted answers for, and John provided the information. Satisfied that everything was in order, she reached across the desk and handed John the contract.

He said, "Great, I'll get this up to legal, and they will put together an 'Author's Package' that describes your rights as the writer and what STP (Small Time Press) is going to do to print and promote your book."

Lynn just sat there nodding like a fool, still not able to believe her good fortune. John gave her the pay schedule and Lynn asked, "What is this?"

"Oh, that is the price we are going to charge for your book. The hardbacks will sell for $24.99 and the paperbacks will sell for $12.99." John replied, with a smile.

Lynn started to do the math in her head, when John reached across the desk and handed Lynn a piece of paper. It was a check for fifty thousand dollars. Lynn just sat there and looked at it.

John told her, "This should cover the first printing and the signing tour. We have you scheduled at bookstores in Provincetown Massachusetts, Boston, Hartford Connecticut, New York, Newark New Jersey, and Philadelphia."

Lynn sat there stupefied, and said, "But how did you know that I would even sign the contract?"

John smiled sheepishly and said, "Oh I had a little bird tell me that you did."

Lynn shook her head and asked, "That little bird wouldn't be named Jewel would it?"

John chuckled and said, "Trust me Lynn; she has your best interests at heart."

Lynn put the check in her purse and almost had to pinch herself. John took her on a tour of their facility. He showed her a room full of drafting tables with people hunched over drawing pictures on assorted colored paper. He introduced her to a girl named Sally and stated that Sally would be doing the artwork for her dust jacket and paperbacks. John then led her through to large swinging doors and she found herself in an industrial room with ten printing presses of various sizes, all of which were humming and spitting out pages of books. He told her that her book would probably be 4 inches wide by 7 and half inches long, which is the average size of any paperback. The hardbacks would be 4 inches by 5 inches by 7 inches. He commented that this was small for a hardback but a good size for a book of two hundred or more pages once the typeset was finished. Plus, people tend to buy more books if they are small, less to carry. He showed Lynn the presses that would be printing her books before he took her to the binding department. The binding department was quieter than the printing room but just as busy. He ended the tour with the packaging and shipping department and told her that they had a hundred stores lined up to take 20 copies each except for the hardbacks, those would be sent to the stores that would have her book signings.

He jokingly said, "I hope you have some vacation saved up from job of yours, you're going to need those days for the book tour." Lynn made a mental note to check her vacation time when she returned to work, and speaking of work, she needed to get back to the shop.

She said her goodbyes to John.

In parting, he asked, "So what is your next book going to be about?" Lynn was a little dumbfounded at the question because she hadn't fully digested what was happening with the first book.

All she said was, "I don't know but I'll think of something." Lynn exited the building and walked to her Jeep. She felt different. There sat her Jeep with her bike on the back, but it looked different. She looked up at the sky, it was starting to cloud up but to her, the sky looked different. Everything in her life just changed during the last hour. She went from being a Quality Manager to a published writer with a big check in her purse in just one short hour. She couldn't breathe. Again, that surreal feeling overcame her. She climbed into her Jeep as the first sign of rain drops hit her windshield, but for the first time, the rain didn't bother her. She was on her way.

The following weeks were a flurry of activity with artwork to approve, legal documents and waivers to sign, and of course, seeing her first book in print. She ear marked the first book to go to the Duck, but she didn't have Duck's address, they had only corresponded electronically so she made a note to get the woman's address so she could send her a signed copy. The second copy went to Jewel for had it not been for her, she wouldn't be holding a book in her hand. She had been given ten hardback copies to give as gifts but she didn't have ten people to give them to, she thought of Frank but didn't want to dash his hopes by giving him a lesbian love story. So she carried them around in her Jeep just in case she ran into someone who would appreciate her literature. She laughed at herself, "My literature? Really Lynn? You think you're Hemingway now?"

Her first book signing was in Provincetown, Massachusetts and she was glad to have it in a place that was familiar to her. She liked P-Town and came here a couple of times every summer just to hang out, eat oysters, buy pullovers, and take in a show. The bookstore was small and on Commercial Street, she had been in the store many times before so she knew it well. She drove the two hours from her house to the large parking lot where she could park all day for twenty dollars. She made the short walk to the bookstore and ran into John. She asked him, "What are you doing here?" He replied, "I wouldn't miss your first book signing." He had arrived earlier and helped the owner of the bookstore set up a table outside on the sidewalk that ran in front of the store. He had piled up two stacks of books for her to sign as he sold them. He said that in the future, the signings would be inside and there would be attendants helping her. He had brought 15 copies with him and just as Lynn sat down; a couple approached the table and picked up a book. They leafed through it, with one woman reading over the shoulder of the other woman. They read the front of the dust jacket and then the back, and one of the women said, "Oh Gosh, you wrote this?"

Lynn turned three shades of red and said, "Yes, I wrote it."

The other woman said, "Honey, I think we should buy this book." And with that, Lynn sold her first book to a woman named Leslie.

Lynn wrote, "To Leslie, Thank you for being the first buyer of my book. Warm Regards, Lynn Tunney." She was on her way! Within an hour, Lynn and John had sold all of the books on the table plus the ones that she had been carrying around in her Jeep. Autographed books were sold at $30.00 each so John left with over $700.00 dollars and high hopes that there would be a second printing. Lynn left with no money because she had already been paid but what she did leave with was priceless. Her heart was filled with pride as to what she had accomplished. After the book signing, she walked across the street and ordered a dozen Russian Oysters and an ice water with lime. It was a good day.

The next two months had Lynn traveling down the East Coast in her Jeep to book signings. She had one every two weeks and usually on a Saturday. She had a good run in Boston and once again sold out all of her hardback copies plus all of the paperbacks the store had ordered. John was going to make back his money in no time she thought. Plus she had heard that the e-book was selling at a phenomenal rate. Her contract said she would gross 65% of online sales and the last time she looked her bank account she had over ten thousand dollars and she knew that was six thousand more than what her paychecks added up to be. She was amazed. After her book signing in Hartford Connecticut, a group of women lingered around and asked Lynn if she wanted to go out for drinks. She didn't drink but went with the women anyway. She followed the women to a bar in downtown Hartford and when they walked in, the women in the lead said, "Here she is. This is the book writer I was telling you about." Several women on barstools turned around, smiled brightly and offered to buy Lynn any drink she wanted. Lynn politely ordered a club soda with lime and a cup of coffee. She spent the rest of the night talking to women who wanted to know the "real" story about Annie. Lynn shared more details than what was written in the book and she had a captive audience. By the end of the night, the women had a few choice words to say about Annie and how she just stopped communicating with Lynn. Lynn tried to defend Annie by saying that she probably just got scared or something and couldn't handle her own feelings.

Two weeks later, she found herself in the heart of Greenwich Village on the island of Manhattan. Again, there was another sell out of books. In Newark she was asked to read and answer questions, which she did. It never ceased to amaze her how people thought of Annie as a bad seed. Even though Lynn would say, "Annie is the reason there is a book at all, we should thank her instead of criticize her." Newark was the toughest crowd yet but she successfully sold all of her hardbacks plus all of the paperbacks. She drove the long drive back to her cabin in the woods and thought about her next book. She wondered if she could do it, or was she a one hit wonder and didn't have another book in her. The drives to the book signings were long and gave her time to think. She thought about Annie and wondered where she was, what she was doing, and if she, by chance, had seen the book. She would have to ask John if there were any bookstores in Albuquerque carrying her book. Not that it mattered, it had been almost a year since she lost contact with Annie and didn't think that she gave her a second thought. Her last book signing was coming up and it would take her to the City of Brotherly Love. Lynn thought it ironic that she would end her book tour in the very city that Annie had grown up. Lynn researched the archives of her mind and remembered that Annie had said that she had an Aunt and Uncle that still lived there. Lynn then wondered why she was even thinking about Annie and her family

Annie had spent the same three months wandering aimlessly through life. Her kids scored really high on the scholastic exams and she was very proud of them. Milton, the class ferret, was beginning to put on weight and there was a raffle to see who would take him home for the summer and of course, Earl won the raffle and he cried from joy of having his little friend with him for three whole months. Annie continued to run her three miles a day and was able to get back into her dance studio; she thought of Lynn on a daily basis. She couldn't help but think of her and how close they had become during their months of chatting. Then she got scared. She was not scared of Lynn but more scared of her own feelings for Lynn.

One day she decided she needed to get out of the condo. It was raining, which is rare for Albuquerque, so she opted for the mall which would help her get her steps in. She had recently starting walking in addition to her running and everything she read told her ten thousand steps a day was a good number. She also thought she could pass the time window shopping. She put on a pair of shorts, a blouse, and her sneakers and went to her car. She drove to the mall and noticed that she needed new windshield wipers. It hardly ever rained so she determined the wipers failed due to sun rather than rain. She parked by the food court and made her way into the "maul", another term she had bestowed the shopping environment instead of mall.

She passed through the food court which was mixture smells from the Chinese fast food; the pizza restaurant; the cinnamon roll store; and the Mexican buffet. The mixture of odors made her stomach roll but not in a good way. She picked up her pace and turned right to the location of some of her favorite clothing boutiques and the book store that she liked to frequent. She passed Talbots and saw a skirt that she liked, but liked the sandals the mannequin was wearing better. She perused the candle shop and looked for a new pair of running shoes. As she was passing the book store, a title caught her eye, so she entered and started hunting for section that she thought would contain the book. She was passing a large table with a sign on it that said, "Up and Coming Authors". She stopped dead in her tracks, staring at a book titled, "The Teacher and The Squid" by Terry Perry. She almost lost her breath and her head began to spin. Oh my Gosh! Did Lynn write a book about them, but who was this Terry Perry maybe it was her pen name? During their conversations in the chat room, Lynn had mentioned that she always wanted to write a book but she never would've thought that she would write a book about THEM! She forgot about the book on display, picked up the Lynn's small book, and headed to the register. She couldn't get home fast enough.

She raced home, screeched to a stop in her parking spot, and bounded up the stairs to her condo. She hung up her keys, dropped her purse, grabbed a bottle of water from the fridge and sat down on the couch to read what Lynn had to say. The first four chapters were about Lynn and the second four were about Annie. Lynn didn't chat much about her work and even though the book was fiction, it detailed the pressure that Annie never knew that Lynn was under. She liked the parts when Lynn rode her bike and the book described more than Lynn ever shared in the chat room. After the first four chapters, she thought that she knew Lynn a little better and that her integrity came through her written words. Annie continued to read and what Lynn had said about her was not far from the truth. Lynn was able to interpret their chats almost exactly and how she portrayed Annie was both respectful and accurate. Tears came to her eyes when she got to the part of the book in which Lynn wrote about her feelings for Annie. She never really took Lynn seriously but here it was, in black and white. She finished the book before she finished her bottle of water. It was a quick read but a good read. She was impressed with Lynn and her ability to write a love story when all she had ever read were Lynn's short sentences in the chat room. She held the little book in her hands and sadly thought to herself, "I let her go."

Annie returned to the kitchen to recycle her water bottle and went to lie down. She needed a nap or rather she just needed to meditate on what she had read, she took the book with her. After an about an hour of going back and forth between her thoughts and re-reading parts of the book, she drifted off to sleep. She awoke when she heard her phone ring. It was her Aunt calling to see if Annie had booked her flight to come back east and see her and her Uncle. Annie replied yes and went back to the kitchen where she had her flight info paper clipped to her calendar and gave her Aunt her flight number and itinerary to Philadelphia. She put Lynn's book in her purse and would read parts of it daily just to be close to Lynn; Annie had no idea as to how to contact Lynn again. She knew that Lynn no longer went into the chat room but then again, neither did she.

By the time that Lynn had made it to Philadelphia, her book was flying off of the shelves and kept the internet buzzing. John had called her right before she left and said that a second printing was scheduled during the next month and that she could expect another royalty check and that her book would be picked up by Barnes & Noble for mass distribution. She couldn't wrap her brain around that right now, she needed to get to Philly and sign some books. She pulled into the parking lot of Books a Million and noticed that a line had formed both inside and outside the store. John made sure she had another hundred copies in hardback just for this store; it was going to be her biggest signing to date. She got out of her Jeep and walked up to the door of the store and all of a sudden, women started clapping. Lynn couldn't get used to the applause and it had started in Greenwich Village. She put on her brightest smile, waved to the crowd and walked into the store. When Lynn approached the signing table she noticed that John had gone all out for this show. There was a bigger than life photo of Lynn behind the table and Lynn was suddenly embarrassed. She would never get used to the fame that this little book had brought. There were canvas book bags being sold that had the picture from the dust jacket silk screened to each side. There were little stuffed squids decorating the table and more in the boxes that were stored behind the huge photo of Lynn. She had three attendants at this signing; one that sold the book bags, one that sat at the table taking money for books and little squids, and one that made sure that all supplies were restocked when they started getting low. Every book bag was sold, all but one squid was sold, and of course all of the books were gone. The book signing took over four hours to complete because Lynn always made it a point to acknowledge the person buying the book and making sure that each message that accompanied the autograph was well thought out and unique. Lynn was exhausted by the time it was over.

There were no books left on the table when Lynn had left to go to the bathroom. When she returned she just sat down without noticing the woman who had walked up to the table and picked up the last little squid. She was tired and cursed herself for not getting a hotel room. She grew even wearier when she thought about the long ride back to her little cabin in the woods. Lynn was down to one remaining attendant and she had gone to order Lynn a cup of coffee from the bistro inside the bookstore. Without looking up, Lynn pulled the woman's book in front of her, she noticed that it was worn and dog eared on certain pages. She picked up her pen and turned to the blank page at the beginning of the book. She asked, "Who do I make this out to?" The woman said, "The Teacher." Lynn began to write and after she finished the first two words, "The Teacher" she stopped writing and just looked at the blank page in front of her as tears welled in her eyes. She swallowed hard, smiled, and slowly looked up into the warm soft hazel eyes of the woman standing before her. Annie returned the smile with her own tears and said, "Hello Squid".